The New Pete

by Jane Sorenson

STANDARD PUBLISHING
Cincinnati, Ohio

2986

Library of Congress Cataloging-in-Publication Data

Sorenson, Jane.
  The new Pete.

  (A Jennifer book ; 9)
  Summary: Anxious to be accepted by the popular crowd,
Pete makes several attempts at changing his image before
finding his true place.
  [1. Popularity—Fiction. 2. Self-perception—
Fiction] I. Title. II. Series: Sorenson, Jane.
Jennifer book ; 9.
PZ7.S7214Ne 1986   [Fic]   86-5753
ISBN 0-87403-086-2

With love to my daughter-in-law
Amanda Sorenson

and a loving welcome to
Caitlin Elizabeth Sorenson,
my first grandchild

Chapter 1

Welcome Home, Jennifer!

Lord, it's me, Jennifer.

Our week in Haiti was over, and Grandma and I were flying back to Miami. We'd be splitting up there because she was heading for her condo on the Gulf, and I was going home to Philadelphia. Frankly, it seems like I've lived in Philadelphia forever, even though we moved less than a year ago.

Everybody coming back into the United States from a trip overseas has to go through customs. But Grandma and I had a plan. It was her idea. We were going to beat the system. Stand in endless lines? Not us!

During our flight from Haiti to Miami, we had filled out our customs forms. That means we each made a list of everything we had bought to bring back into the United States. For example, my Haitian doll.

"Each tourist is allowed to bring back $400 worth of purchases duty-free," Grandma said. "In other words, without paying a tax."

"You've got to be kidding," I laughed. "I still have most of my travelers' checks in my purse." I had spent a grand total of $19.30 on gifts and souvenirs. Grandma hadn't spent much more.

"My friends tell me it's easier to spend money in other countries. Things cost more, and there's more to tempt you!" Grandma smiled.

By now, the plane had landed, and we stood in the aisle. "Are you sure you can carry the luggage?" Grandma wondered.

"I can make several trips," I assured her. Our plan was that she would rush right over to stand in a customs line and I would bring over our luggage as soon as I got it off the carousel. The Miami airport was jammed with people. But Grandma was about tenth in line. She can move fast.

"All right!" said the man standing next to me, as he grabbed a large basket from the revolving track. When his suitcase appeared, he rushed over to stand behind Grandma. Suddenly a whole surge of luggage came through at once, and all the travelers were grabbing. It seemed like everybody found their bags except me. I couldn't believe it. I glanced toward Grandma. She waved. Tourists were carrying and dragging stuff over into the customs lines. What if Grandma's turn came and I was still waiting? I was starting to sweat.

"I haven't seen either suitcase," a man near me said. I looked up. Although his wife was wearing diamond stud earrings, she didn't look pretty. "Of course, I've been watching!" The man talked louder. "If you don't believe me, *you* try standing here a while!" I guess she believed him. They stood and waited nervously. His wife glanced at her watch. "Our connecting flight leaves in half an hour!" she said. He nodded.

I leaned to one side to see how Grandma was coming. She was next in line! I waved and shook my head. I watched her step aside to let others go through the line ahead of her.

Well, there's no use dragging on the suspense any longer. By the time the baggage carousel was empty again, Grandma had joined me. So much for our plan. As You know, sometimes even the greatest plans mess up. Do You realize it ahead of time?

"It's no use," a young woman sighed. "They just aren't here!" I realized that ours weren't the only missing suitcases.

In the beginning, when I first started flying, I worried about my suitcase getting lost. But it had never happened before. Come to think of it, on this very trip I had been uncomfortable about having my luggage checked through from Philadelphia to Haiti. That meant the suitcase, like me, had to change planes, but I would not be the person to carry it. But, everything had worked out OK—then!

"I'm going to complain to a representative of the airline," said the husband of the cross woman with the diamond earrings. Now she really looked mad.

Grandma and I joined about ten others—all without luggage. Well, some of us had totes, but You know what I mean.

"How can our suitcases get lost when they ride the same plane as us?" I asked.

"Good question, Jennifer," Grandma smiled. "You look upset."

Well, as You know, I'm not good at faking it. "Naturally," I said. "Who wouldn't be? This has never happened to me before!"

Then I realized Grandma was calm. "You had your name and address on your suitcase, didn't you?" she asked.

I nodded. "Yes."

By now the whole group was standing in front of a uniformed woman. "Your luggage must have come on another flight," she explained. "I suggest you complete your travel. At your final destination, you can fill out a complaint describing what's missing."

The people were not happy. "There's nothing *she* can do," explained the husband of the woman in diamond earrings.

"But we've missed our connecting flight!" The earrings sparkled. So did her eyes.

"Let's check *our* schedules." Grandma opened her purse. We sat down and took out our tickets.

"Oh, no!" I said. "My plane is leaving right now! I've

missed it!" Now I really felt upset. "My family is meeting me, and I won't be there! What am I going to do?"

"My flight took off ten minutes ago," Grandma said.

"I always wondered what happens when you miss a plane!"

"Now you know," Grandma said.

I was glad I wasn't alone. "No I don't!" I said.

Grandma smiled. "Has the world come to an end?"

I grinned. "I guess not."

"What's the worst thing that can happen?" she asked.

I thought. "My family would have to wait for me. Will the airline let me get on another plane?"

"Yes," said Grandma. "We'll just take our tickets to the agents, and they'll put us each on the next flight leaving Miami. It doesn't even have to be on the same airline! Traveling by air isn't perfect. Sometimes things *do* go wrong. But the airlines' personnel will take care of us."

"And the suitcases?"

"I'm not sure," Grandma said. "But they must have a system."

I felt a little better. "Why does God let stuff like this happen?" I asked.

"It isn't His fault!" Grandma laughed. "But He can use trouble to teach us lessons. Everybody has to learn to handle minor disappointments and stress. Gradually, we learn to handle bigger problems."

"Shall I call my family?"

"That's a good idea, Jennifer," Grandma said. "Let's

get you booked on the next flight out. Then you can tell them when, and what plane to meet."

Once we had our new reservations, Grandma helped me use her credit card to call home. She said it was easier than standing at the phone and feeding in coins. The line was busy! I couldn't believe it! Well, that's not entirely true. But usually I'm the one that's talking!

I finally got through. "Dad, it's me, Jennifer!" The family was just getting ready to drive to the airport. I told Dad the time and number of my new flight. "I'm anxious to see you too," I said.

Well, Lord, that's how I mostly missed going through customs on my first trip home from another country. A large customs inspector poked through my tote and shook his head. And that was it!

Grandma and I didn't have much time to say good-bye. "Thanks for taking me to Haiti," I said. "I'll never forget it!"

"I won't either, Jennifer." She hugged me. "Give your family my love!" I promised I would.

* * * * * * * *

As I sat looking out the window of the huge plane on the way to Philadelphia, I realized that sometimes things do go wrong in the United States. But most people don't *expect* to miss planes or have their luggage get lost. Usually, things go as scheduled. And, when they don't, we complain.

How different from Haiti! There, people *expect* things to go wrong. And they often do! But if there's no rain and the crops fail, the Haitian farmers are sure next year will be better! How can they be so patient?

I looked down at the highways, the telephone poles, the even shapes of the farm fields. For the first time in my life I realized that nearly everybody has a phone, and a car, and equipment to do the heavy work.

I looked down, and I remembered the Haitian island of La Gonave. From the air it would look like a rock pile! No paved roads. No telephones. Hardly any cars. In fact, hardly any pure water!

I looked down at the houses. From the plane, they looked like little boxes. But I knew that, up close, most of them had at least several rooms, electricity, and toilets. In my mind, I could still see Haitian's falling-down shacks, the slums, the filth.

"What do you mean, you don't have any more sirloin tips!" a man yelled at the flight attendant. The passengers near me didn't even look up from their magazines.

"Thank you," I said, when my meal was handed to me. I remembered starving Haitian children. I remembered the one-meal-a-day given to the lucky kids enrolled in schools.

Then, for the very first time in my life, when I thanked You for my food, it wasn't just a habit! You know, like "Whose turn to pray?" Or "Hurry, or the food will get cold." I'll never again take meals for granted!

After the attendant removed my tray, I looked down at

the United States. Do You ever do that, Lord? I mean, do You look down at our whole country from Heaven? When I looked down from the airplane, I realized how fortunate we are. Do You ever do that, Lord?

Chapter 2

Culture Shock

Lord, it's me, Jennifer.

As my plane flew north from Florida, darkness and winter returned at about the same time. I had forgotten about winter, but now I started hoping Mom would remember to bring my warm coat to the airport. I'd look pretty dumb in my cotton skirt and blouse. Not to mention that I'd probably freeze to death!

Down in Haiti, it is always summer. Hot or hotter. Only in the mountains does it really cool off. I was returning to a world of furnaces and air conditioning, shade and screened-in porches. In the United States, being uncomfortable because of the weather isn't permitted! And for my entire life, I had taken that for granted.

I turned on the light above my seat and reached for my purse. I had saved the best for last. Sort of like eating the cake out of the middle and then pigging out on pure chocolate frosting. There it was; my picture of Kirlene!

Lord, out of all the kids in Haiti, did You pick out Kirlene for me to sponsor? Do You do things like that? I kinda think You do bring people together. I wish I could have actually met her before I had to go home. But we can get to know each other through letters. And someday, I'll go back to see her!

I looked at the picture and into Kirlene's eyes. It was hard to tell what she was like. Yet, somehow, I was going to change her world!

Me! Well, naturally I can't change the *whole* world! But I can change Kirlene's world. That is, if I can figure out a way to earn $21 a month. Lord, please show me how to do that!

"Please place your seat in an upright position," the flight attendant told me. I felt embarrassed. I hadn't even heard the announcement. I realized we were landing in Philadelphia.

You are supposed to keep your seat belts fastened until the plane comes to a stop. As usual, lots of people were standing up getting stuff from the overhead compartments. I was tempted to do the same thing. After all, what could happen now? But I didn't do it. As You know, my parents are big on following the rules.

"Hi, Jennifer!" Justin yelled so loud that people looked at me. Some of them smiled.

I waited until I got closer to my family. "Hi, everybody," I said.

14

"How was Haiti?" Dad asked.

"Fantastic," I said.

"And how is Grandma?" Mom wanted to know.

"Wonderful!" I said. Everyone laughed because Grandma Green says "Wonderful" a lot.

"Let's get your luggage," Dad said. "We can talk in the car on the way home. Have you eaten?"

"I had supper on the plane," I said. "But my suitcase got lost between Haiti and Miami."

"Oh, no," Mom said.

"That doesn't happen often," Dad said. "Well, we'll just have to fill out a form at the baggage claim area."

"Back to winter, I see!" Since it's January, naturally everybody was wearing winter coats. I felt really stupid with my bare arms hanging out. But Mom was holding my navy blue coat. "How come you brought that one?" I asked. Before she could answer, I caught sight of my brother, Pete. He's in sixth grade. I saw him, but I couldn't believe my eyes.

Pete stood apart from the rest of the family, sort of leaning against the wall. He was wearing sunglasses. And earphones. And the strangest haircut I've ever seen! The fact that his gym shoes were untied wasn't keeping him from bopping around to a beat only he could hear.

Mom and Dad didn't say anything. They were ignoring him. That was obvious. And Pete was ignoring the whole family. In fact, he was ignoring the whole world.

I glanced at Justin and nodded at the new Pete. I think I raised my eyebrows. That's what I was trying to do, anyhow. Justin, who's in fourth grade, but about a head shorter than Pete, rolled his eyes. I felt like laughing. In fact, I felt perilously close to hysteria. But it was clear that Dad wasn't amused. So I took a deep breath and followed my parents. I knew I didn't dare look at Justin or we'd both explode.

"Hey, hey, Jenny!" Pete muttered, as I passed. Nobody's ever called me that in my life. "Back to the real world, I see!"

I've never talked to anybody wearing headphones before. I didn't know if he could hear me or not. So I nodded.

"Did you get lots of pictures?" Justin asked.

"I sure did! Thanks for letting me use your new camera!" We were walking side by side. "I don't want to turn around," I said. "Is Pete coming?"

Justin glanced around and nodded. "Mr. Cool!"

"I can't believe it," I said. "Not Pete!"

"Believe it," my youngest brother said.

Pete has always been kind of square. Not exactly a loser, but not a winner either. But he's always *looked* pretty normal. Except, of course, when he was forced to do anything athletic.

Dad turned around. "Hope I'm not walking too fast," he said.

I shook my head. Then, when Dad wasn't looking, I glanced over my shoulder. Pete, the Cool, was sort of boogieing down the red carpet. "I'm going to laugh," I told Justin.

16

"No, you aren't," he said. He was right.

"What happened to him?"

"See for yourself!" Justin said. "I'll fill you in later."

I noticed a few startled looks as we proceeded through the airport. I found myself pretending not to know Pete either! Frankly, his behavior wasn't cool. It was more like weird. I was actually relieved when we got to the baggage claim area.

"Blue American Tourister," I told the airline representative. I had to look in my purse for the flight number and my baggage claim ticket.

"That's all there is to it," the man said, looking up from the claim form.

"What will happen?" I asked.

"Your luggage should be delivered to your home tomorrow."

"No kidding?" I said.

The man smiled. "No kidding!"

Pete stood near a post and looked cool. Well, to be honest, he really looked weird. But I've said that before, and You probably noticed Yourself anyway.

"Can't you even say hello to your sister?" Dad asked Pete. Our station wagon was on the second parking level.

Pete nodded once. "I did," he said. Then he climbed into the seat facing the rear.

"Well, Jennifer, tell us all about Haiti," Mom said, in what sounded like a desperate attempt at cheerfulness. She can't stand tension.

"I hardly know where to begin," I started out. "It's a

totally different world. Not like the pictures in your cruise folders. At least, most of Haiti isn't a tropical paradise any longer." I felt disloyal. "I mean, it's beautiful where there's enough water."

Dad threaded his way onto the expressway. Nobody said anything. I guess they were waiting for me to tell them all about my trip. But I couldn't. At least, not then. "I'm really tired," I said. "How about if I save my report for later?"

Sitting in the dark in our car, I felt as if I had just come back from the moon! I watched the expensive cars, the big buildings, the smooth roads. How could I describe Haiti's beautiful, generous people, who share what little they have? How could I describe that falling-down shack, where a tiny widow prayed for *me?* How could I describe the feeling of guilt when I realized that my horse gets better care than most of Haiti's children? How could I describe children who can't go to school because they don't have money for a uniform and books?

"Haiti must have made quite an impression," Dad said. "I can't remember many times when you've been speechless." I had the feeling that Dad understood.

"Some of the people in Haiti have a lot of money," I said. "They have big cars and swimming pools and everything. But *most* of the people are very poor!" Suddenly, tears welled up in my eyes.

"Lots of the world is like that," Dad said. "In fact, there's plenty of poverty right here in the United States."

I had never thought much about it. I knew Dad was

right, but right now I couldn't deal with that too. So I just sat in the car and felt bombarded by civilization.

"It's probably jet lag," Mom said, knowingly.

I remember hearing about *culture shock*. For me, seeing Haiti was mostly an adventure. Now, for some reason, I'm more blown away coming back to civilization!

At last we turned into our driveway. Dad pushed a button, and the electric garage door went up. A light automatically turned on in the garage. I was home.

Chapter 3

Pete's Bombshell

Lord, it's me, Jennifer.

To be honest, I was so much into seeing stuff and learning about Haiti, I practically forgot about things at home. Somehow I expected life to stand still and wait for me. But it didn't. I guess it never does.

The phone started ringing while I was hanging up my coat. Would it be Matthew Harrington or Mack? Or Heidi Stoltzfus? Or, of course! It would be Chris McKenna, telling me all about Star, my new horse! I stood in the front hall waiting to be called to the phone.

There I stood. Nothing happened. I strolled into the kitchen. Pete was draped across the floor with his feet balanced on the edge of a chair. I nearly stepped on him.

"Watch it, Jenny!" he said. Then he returned to his conversation. "Just my sister," I heard him say, softly.

I turned around and headed down to the family room. "What's with Pete?" I asked Mom.

"I'm not exactly sure," she said. "I guess it's just a new stage." See, Mom has this theory that kids are programmed like a computer. The "stages" started when we were babies, and I'm not sure if they'll ever end. Is she right, Lord?

"Thought maybe you'd like a little fire!" Dad, his arms full of logs, tracked into the room. "I'll bet you nearly forgot about winter, didn't you?" He grinned.

"Correct," I admitted.

"Need some help, Dad?" Justin offered. I mean, he wasn't even asked! Together, he and Dad arranged the kindling and paper just the way Dad likes it. The logs went on top.

"Don't forget to open the flue," Mom reminded. A flue is a passageway inside the chimney that lets the smoke out. If it's closed, the house fills with smoke.

"How's that for a nice fire?" Dad bragged.

"Anybody for ice cream?" Mom asked.

"Sounds good," I admitted. "Want me to help, Mom?" I hadn't been asked either, as You probably noticed. Is being helpful *catching?*

"Just relax," Mom said. "You said you're tired. Right?"

"Well," I admitted, "I'm not *that* tired. I could help."

"Stay put, Dear," she said.

"Hey," I asked, "what time *is* it."

"About 7:30," Dad said.

22

I stopped to figure it out. "Saturday night, right?"

"You've got it," Justin said.

"How come everybody's home?" I asked.

"It was Dad's idea," Justin said. "You know, *family night!* Sort of like in the olden days."

"What do you mean 'olden days,' Justin?" Dad grinned. "Can't a family spend time together without it being a big deal?"

"Dad," I asked, "did you make everybody stay home tonight because I was coming home? I can't believe it."

My father laughed. "Not exactly," he admitted.

"You said we all had to go to the airport," Justin said.

"True," Dad admitted.

Mom came in with a tray filled with dishes of ice cream. "There's strawberry, chocolate almond, and Dutch apple."

"No chocolate chocolate chip?" Dad complained.

"You finished that off the other night," Mom reminded him.

"Where's Pete?" Dad asked. I looked at Mom.

"Talking on the phone," she said.

"Justin, tell him his time is up," Dad said.

"Why me?"

"Just lucky, I guess," Dad said.

"If I'm not back before my ice cream starts to melt, send a rescue squad," Justin said.

Well, my brothers came into the room. Together. They weren't even punching each other. I couldn't believe it.

"Dibbs on the strawberry," Justin said.

"Strawberry's for kids," Pete told him.

"Then *you* take it," Justin offered. I relaxed. This was more like it.

"No way," Pete announced. He selected the chocolate almond and sprawled on the floor. Frankly, it's a good thing our family room is so big. As it was, Pete filled up most of the floor space. When did he get so tall?

It was awfully quiet. I mean, you could hear our spoons clicking on the dishes.

"Maybe we could watch TV," Pete suggested.

"What's on?" Justin asked.

"Wait a minute," Dad said. "Are you trying to say that we aren't capable of entertaining ourselves?"

"Even the Waltons had a radio," Justin reminded him.

"How long has this been going on?" I asked. "Dad's latest stage, I mean?"

Mom chuckled. "I'm not sure. Could we play a game, Peter?"

"Another time," Dad said. "Tonight is for family conversation."

Pete groaned. "Wait till I tell Scott this!"

"Scott who?" I asked.

"Scott Franklin. You know, the guy who was here a lot last summer. Lives down past Harringtons." I kind of remembered. But not too well.

"OK," Dad said. "We seem to need a little structure. Why don't we each ask Jennifer a question about Haiti?" He looked at me. "Are you revived enough to answer a few questions?"

24

"Sure," I said. I mean, it was either that or total Dulls-ville! Maybe I'd get lucky and the phone would ring!

"I'll start," Justin said. "Did you and Grandma ride horses up to the Citadelle?"

"We did," I laughed. I told them about our legs dangling down. And how we were wearing skirts. And how we each had a boy pulling the horse in front and another switching him from behind. "And it was right on the edge of the mountain!"

"Was the fort as huge as in the pictures?" Pete asked.

"I think it was even bigger!" I said.

"What surprised you the most?" Dad asked.

I had to stop and think a minute. The poverty? It was worse than I expected. The contrast between the rich and the poor? The fact that most kids don't go to school? There had been so many surprises!

"That's hard to answer," I said. "This may sound dumb. But I think I just figured it out. In Haiti, for the first time, I realized that God isn't an American!"

Everyone just looked at me. Then Pete said, "Heavy!"

"Hmmmm," Dad said. "I think I see what you mean."

"I don't," said Justin. Frankly, I didn't care whether Justin understood or not—even *I* needed to think more about it. Later, in private.

Mom kept things moving with her attempted cheerfulness. "Did you buy anything?" she asked.

"Not too much," I said. "But I have little gifts for everybody. Some stuff is in my suitcase, though. You'll have to wait till it comes."

"What did you miss most?" Pete asked. "Or maybe I should ask *who?*"

"Think I'd tell you?" I laughed. "I guess I missed having pure water! We just take it for granted. But you should see the guck some people have to drink! Even in hotels, Grandma and I couldn't brush our teeth with water from the faucet!"

Lord, I didn't plan *not* to tell them about Kirlene, but I want it to be the right time. Maybe tomorrow.

"Even having ice cream and a refrigerator would be impossible in most of Haiti," I said. "By the way, the ice cream was great, Mom!"

"Thanks, Jennifer."

The fire had died down. Even I had to admit that sitting here with my family was kind of special. And the phone didn't ring at all. Probably everybody was at a game or something.

"What's been going on here?" I asked.

"Oh, the usual," Justin grinned.

"We were all invited to an open house at Harringtons for New Year's Day," Mom said. "People watched the football games if they wanted to. Or played games. Or just visited."

"The food was excellent," Dad said. And my brothers agreed.

"Sorry I missed it," I said. I really am! But no matter what people think, you can't have it *all*.

"The house was full of people," Mom said. "There were several whole families from the church."

"Really?" I said. "Like who?"

"Oh, the Stoltzfus family. And Williamses, Spencers," Justin recited.

"Don't forget the minister," Pete added. "The whole Robbins family was there."

"Mrs. Williams wore her new wig," Mom said. I thought about Mrs. Williams' beautiful hair, and how it had fallen out when she started treatments for her cancer.

"You could hardly tell it wasn't her own hair!" Mom continued.

"I could," Pete said.

"I didn't think you noticed anybody except Kristen Robbins," Justin said.

Well! *That* was news to me! Pete's never noticed any girl before! Not that I'm aware of. How about that!

"Too bad she didn't notice you!" Justin added.

"Enough!" Dad said. "It was a great party."

"Because your teams won!" Mom said.

"No. It would have been good anyhow." He grinned. "Well, maybe not quite as good!"

"Why don't you start your showers?" Mom suggested. "Jennifer, would you like to use the master bathroom?"

"Sounds excellent," I said.

"By the way," Pete said, as he stood up and stretched. "I'm not going to Sunday school tomorrow."

A bomb dropped on our house wouldn't have had as dramatic an effect! We all stopped right in the middle of what we were doing.

Dad stopped closing the glass doors in front of the

fireplace and turned around. "What did you say, Pete?"

"I said I'm not going to Sunday school tomorrow."

"I don't know what you're trying to prove," Dad said slowly. "But this is not the way to do it. You will go to Sunday school tomorrow just as you always do."

"You can't make me," Pete said.

Lord, I thought maybe You'd strike him blind. Or speechless. Or, in case You didn't, Dad probably would! I, and the rest of the family, waited.

"Pete, I'd much prefer that you go to Sunday school because you want to," Dad told him. "But, if that's not the case, you'll go because *I* want you to. Whether you like it or not, I'm in charge here."

"But Dad . . ."

"That's it for now," Dad said. "When the Harringtons arrive in the morning, you'll be ready." He spoke with his no-nonsense voice. Then he relaxed, turned to me, and smiled. "Welcome home, Jennifer!" he said. And he walked right over and gave me a big hug. I nearly fainted.

Chapter 4

Two Visitors

Lord, it's me, Jennifer.

When I went up to my room and turned on the light, I suddenly realized that I have been taking a lot for granted. My room looks like something out of a storybook. Lord, how do You decide who gets mud walls and who gets a private room with Laura Ashley wallpaper?

I undressed, put on a robe, and went into my parents' bathroom. How do You decide which people get no bathrooms and which families get *three?*

For the first time, I really noticed the shower. Three walls are white ceramic tile, and the one with the door is glass. Naturally, you can't see through it. With just one hand, I pulled on the faucet and sort of dialed the right temperature. It never impressed me until tonight. And the water. It's what people call *soft* water. That means it slides over you and doesn't leave soapy scum. Some water is soft all by itself. Ours in Illinois wasn't soft, so we had an appliance that did the trick. It had something to do with huge bags of salt.

As I lathered the fragrant soap and shampoo, I thought about the stinky brown water in Bat Cave in Haiti! Lord, thanks for this lovely, clean water!

When I got back to my room, I was surprised to see that Justin was already there.

"What's with Pete?" I asked.

"It might be sort of a New Year's resolution," Justin explained. "He told me that this year he was going to stop being a nerd. Or wimp. Whatever."

I sat on the edge of my bed. We aren't supposed to sit on our beds, but I didn't think Justin would notice, and, if he did, he'd never rat on me. Besides, he was making himself comfortable in my beanbag chair.

"Did something happen at the Harringtons' party?" I asked. "You know, something that put Pete down?"

"I'm not sure," my brother said. "There were so many kids there and so much was going on. Besides, I was mostly with Keever." As You know, Keever is my friend Heidi's younger brother.

"Besides Mike Harrington, who were the other sixth-graders there?" I asked.

"Jamie Williams," he said.

"Right. And Megan Spencer," I remembered. Her mom's my Sunday-school teacher.

"And Kristin Robbins, of course. Every time I saw

30

Pete, he was watching her," Justin said. Our minister's daughter. Your typical extravert. Cute. Mostly because she doesn't realize it yet. Bouncy. Probably a cheerleader in a few years. "Do you think she knew Pete was watching her?"

"Nah." Justin shook his head. "She doesn't know boys exist. You know, as in, *boyfriends*. She was having too much fun with everybody at the party."

"That's all?" I asked. "Were Mike Harrington and Pete the only sixth grade guys?"

"Not at Sunday school. But we're talking about people who were invited to Harringtons' party," Justin explained.

"Right," I remembered. I had only been gone a week. "What happened *before* the party? You know, during the days after I left for Haiti?"

"Nothing," Justin said. "How should I know?"

"You were here."

"Cool it," he said. "I don't spend all my time playing detective with Pete! Who needs it?"

"I'm sorry," I said. "I just wondered if you happened to notice anything unusual."

"Just the clothes and stuff."

"How did that start?"

"Pete and Scott Franklin went to the mall to spend their Christmas money." Justin yawned.

"Scott is the kid in the neighborhood?"

"Right." Suddenly, he stood up. "Gotta go." The shower had just turned off, which had to mean that Pete would be coming out of the other bathroom. "See ya," Justin said, as he slipped out the door.

I soon found out that unpacking without a suitcase doesn't take long. I tried to remember what I was missing. Mostly summer clothes, and I didn't need them anyhow. Not in Philadelphia in January!

I was opening my closet to pick out something to wear to church when I thought of my Bible—it was in my suitcase. Maybe I could borrow one. Unfortunately, in our house there aren't a lot of Bibles to spare.

I smiled as I remembered the time I took our huge family Bible to a youth-group meeting. That was last year, before we moved. You remember. Right after my brothers and I first went to Sunday school. At that point we had no choice about going. But lots has happened since then.

There was a knock on my door. I was really surprised. Two visitors in one night! Sometimes I went for weeks without anybody visiting my room. "Come in," I said.

"Hey, man. It's me, Jenny."

"Pete," I said, "you've never called me Jenny before today. In fact, nobody ever has in my whole life."

"So," he said, sprawling in my beanbag chair. "It's a new nickname."

"Well, I'm not so sure I like it," I said. "I prefer being called Jennifer."

"That's life! Sometimes there's no choice," he said.

"What do you mean?"

"Well, for example, somebody in my room at school

decided that all the kids needed nicknames," he told me. "Like Scott Franklin is called 'Fox.' And Jeff is called 'Cool Cantrell.'"

"What do they call Mike Harrington?"

"'Hot Dog,'" Pete said.

I was afraid to ask. "How about you?"

Pete groaned. "I hate to tell you," he said. He paused. "You'll laugh."

"Try me!" I took a deep breath.

"'Saint Peter!'"

I laughed. I couldn't help it. Honestly.

"Cute," my brother said. "Real cute!"

"I'm sorry," I said.

"Do you have any idea how many jokes start out with, *'Have you heard the one about the dog who died and went to Heaven?'* I'm so sick of the pearly gates!"

I could see his point. "Do you think it's because you go to Sunday school?" I asked.

"I guess so."

"Well, Mike goes to Sunday school," I realized.

"Sometimes they call him 'Holy Harrington.' Or 'Halo.'" But there are lots of neat things they call a jock! I'd give anything to be 'Hook' or 'Hunk!'"

Pete looked miserable. Not Mr. Cool. Not sitting there with his striped pajamas hanging on his thin shoulders. And his weird haircut. He sighed. "I guess 'Saint Peter' is better than 'Hippo,'" he said.

"Pete," I asked, "is that why you decided not to go to Sunday school?"

"Well, it's one reason," he said. He climbed out of the chair. "Hey, Jenny, I have to go."

"Jennifer," I said. Slowly and distinctly.

"OK. Jennifer." My other brother stood next to the door. "You know, I'm glad you're back. I kind of missed you." And he was gone.

Wow! Coming from Pete, that was a real compliment. I decided I'd try to help him. But then I remembered another joke with Saint Peter in it and I had another laughing spell.

This thing with Pete was a puzzle, that's for sure. I wondered if I could get used to it if the kids at school started calling me "Jenny."

Then, as I folded back my quilted bedspread, I remembered how wonderful that hot water felt in the shower. And how funny it seemed to be holding my toothbrush under the faucet without fear of getting sick! And how easily I remembered how to blow-dry my hair. I turned my electric blanket to "three" and crawled between the clean sheets.

Lord, please help Pete. And please bless everybody in Haiti, especially Kirlene. Was I really there when I got up this morning? I can hardly believe it. . . .

Chapter 5

Pete's Threads

Lord, it's me, Jennifer.

I woke up suddenly. I had been dreaming that I was taking a bath in Bat Cave, the yuckiest water in Haiti. Actually, the shower was running next door in the "family" bathroom. One of my brothers was already up.

I didn't get out of bed right away. My sheets felt silky and clean, and I was pleasantly warm. Instinctively, I knew my room would be chilly. Dad had begun winter with his seasonal kick to save money on fuel. My room gets the coldest.

Suddenly, I remembered it was Sunday! Excitement overwhelmed me. I was going to see lots of my friends this morning. Well, naturally, I'd be learning more about You! And I hoped that in the afternoon I'd get to see my new horse, Star.

Dad was singing in his shower as I headed down for breakfast. I couldn't recognize the song. That figured. Dad doesn't have to hurry since he and Mom go later for the church service. Which is, of course, why we kids ride to Sunday school with the Harringtons.

"Way to go!" Justin said as I came into the kitchen.

I smiled. But then I realized he wasn't talking to me. I turned around and stood face-to-face with Pete. At first I couldn't say a word.

Well, what *can* you say when your plain, boring brother suddenly turns up looking like a punk rock star? And, on Sunday morning besides. I finally managed a feeble "Wow" before I slipped into my chair.

Words came more quickly to Mom. "I hope you don't think you're going to church looking like that! What would people think?"

Pete sat down and soberly attacked his bowl of custard. After two bites, he looked at Mom. "Dad said I had to go to Sunday school. He didn't say what I had to wear. It's a free country!"

That's what he thinks, I thought. This was getting kind of exciting. Being in the audience is a new role for me. As the oldest, I'm usually on stage.

Justin wasn't saying anything either. But, like me, he was watching with fascination.

"Where did you get those clothes?" Mom asked.

"At the mall. You know, when I went with Scott," Pete said. "I used my own Christmas money!" he explained.

"It isn't respectful," Mom told him. As You know, she

36

has always been big on respect. "People wear their nicest clothes to church."

"Maybe they're trying to impress each other," Pete argued. "What makes you think God cares?"

He had scored a point. And Mom knew it. As we all know, she never went to church at all in her whole life until a few months ago.

"Well, what makes you think God doesn't care?" I asked. As soon as I said it, I was sorry I had gotten involved. Me and my big mouth.

"Get off my case!" Pete said. "It's bad enough having you act like a *parent,* but since when has God appointed *you* to speak for Him?"

"Sorry," I muttered. I decided then and there to stick to watching from the sidelines. It was certainly safer.

"As soon as you finish eating, go up and let your father have a look at you," Mom told Pete.

"I'm finished now," he said. Although he still had several bites left, he stood up.

Nobody said a word. Pete went upstairs. We could hear him knock on Dad's door. I held my breath.

"Well, well," we heard Dad say. "What have we here? Looks like a January trick-or-treater! Do you want Snickers or a Hershey bar?" That's what Dad always asks kids when he answers the door on Halloween.

Pete's voice didn't carry as well. I could tell Mom and Justin couldn't hear either. So we just finished eating.

"Harringtons are due any minute," Pete said from the entry hall. As we joined him, he was putting on his new black jacket over his much-disputed threads. I couldn't believe it.

Justin glanced at me, and we both put on our coats too. Actually, we did look very preppy. Pete, for all the hassle, looked more contemporary.

However, contemporary on a public personality is one thing. Contemporary on your sixth-grade brother is something else. I glanced at Pete one last time and saw his dark shades. Then and there, I decided to pretend I didn't know him.

But ignoring him wasn't easy once we got in the car and Mr. Harrington started to laugh. Frankly, I've never heard grown men laugh that hard except at each other's jokes.

"Hey, Dad, give us a break," Matthew said to his father. "We can't even welcome Jennifer home!" He looked at me and smiled. "Welcome home, world traveler!"

I smiled back. It was easier to ignore Pete once he crawled in beside Mike in the back seat.

"How was Haiti?" Mack asked.

"It was great," I said. "I sure learned a lot." It was hard to give a brief answer to a question like that.

"Mr. Anderson said he's hoping you will tell us about it at a youth-group meeting," Mack said.

"I will, and I hope my pictures turn out," I replied.

"We missed you New Year's Day," Matthew told me.

"I hear you had a great open house."

"It's a family tradition," Mack told us. "We've done it

ever since the Robbins family came to our church."

"You're awfully quiet, Justin," Mark said. He's a high-school senior, who's taken a special interest in my youngest brother.

"Would anybody like to see my pictures of Christmas morning at the Green residence?" Justin asked.

"You wouldn't dare," I said. "Would you?"

"I'm not sure," Justin laughed. "Just testing for reactions."

Well, it was pretty much our usual small talk as we rode through the countryside. When we turned into the parking area, I thought the church building looked cold. Winter had really come to the Valley Forge area. That's for sure.

Once we were inside, it was easy enough for me to avoid Pete. I go to the junior-high department along with Matthew and Mack Harrington. Mr. and Mrs. Harrington go to an adult class. Both my brothers, on the other hand, are in the junior department. Mark Harrington, the high-school senior, is an aid in Justin's fourth-grade class. So lucky Justin, Mike, and Mark all got to walk in with the cool 'Saint Peter.' I didn't even glance at them. I didn't dare.

As I walked into our classroom, I noticed right away that Mr. Williams wasn't in front welcoming everybody like he always does. My first thought was that Mrs. Williams was too sick to be left alone. She's getting chemotherapy treatments for cancer. But, just as I started feeling a knot in my stomach, everyone started clapping and yelling "Welcome Home." Which is what it said on a big poster that reached right across the end of the room. Well, actually it said, "Welcome Home, Jennifer!" I couldn't believe it.

Probably I blushed, cause I know I felt kind of embarrassed. But also, to be honest, I felt very pleased. When you consider I haven't lived here all that long, it was quite an honor. Wouldn't You agree?

When things quieted down, Mr. Williams came up in front. "Some of the kids needed something to do during vacation," he explained. "Making the poster was their idea."

"Thanks a lot!" I said. I hadn't had a chance to sit down.

"Now *this* is *my* idea," Mr. Williams said. "Would you tell us a few impressions of what you saw in Haiti?"

I took a deep breath. "Well . . ." It was a brilliant start! "Haiti is very different from the United States. I don't just mean that Haitians are poor and we're rich. Missionaries told me that Haitians share and help each other. Most of us are very competitive. Me included." The kids laughed.

"Even though they don't have much, the people in Haiti are more contented. No matter what we have, most of us keep wanting more. Me included." They laughed again.

"In Haiti, most people don't have things like electricity, and telephones, and cars, and roads, and clothes, and food, and even water. Here, these things are usually taken for granted." I looked at the kids. "I used to. Take them for granted, that is. But right now I really don't." Nobody laughed.

"Have you ever stopped to think about how many *choices* we have in our country? Restaurants, medicines, colleges, professions, soft drinks. We have so many choices, it's hard to choose. But, in Haiti, most of the people are trapped," I explained. "One missionary said that's what poverty is all about," I said. "Poverty means having no choices."

Nobody clapped when I went to sit with my class. "Thank you, Jennifer," Mr. Williams said. "Let's pray together."

My cheeks felt hot as I bowed my head.

"Lord, how we thank You for reminding us how richly blessed we are in the United States. We thank You for Jennifer's trip and the privilege of sharing what she learned. Bless not only the people of Haiti, but also the people all over the world, particularly those who have few choices. We pray that You will send missionaries to teach them that they can choose to be Your children, through believing in Jesus. In His name, we pray. Amen."

Heidi reached over and squeezed my hand. "Welcome home, sister!" she said.

I grinned. It was good to be back.

Chapter 6

Sparrows and Other Things

Lord, it's me, Jennifer.

As usual, my brothers and I met Mom and Dad after Sunday school. Then our family sits together during church.

"Hi," Dad greeted us. Mom didn't say anything. She seemed tense.

"The junior-high department made me a big welcome sign," I said. "And I got to tell about Haiti."

"That's nice," Mom said. She seemed to be ignoring Pete. He looked just the same as before, except for two things. The part of his hair that used to stick up straight was more plastered down. And he had removed his sunglasses.

I looked at Justin and raised my eyebrows a little. But he just raised his too. What the changes meant, I had no idea. I'd have to wait till later to find out if anything happened during Sunday school. I mean, like anything involving Pete.

"OK," Dad said, leading the way into the sanctuary. We usually sit on the left side toward the back. Personally, I like the front better, but it isn't my choice.

Instead of closing my eyes while the organ played, I looked around. Our church building is beautiful. I was very much aware of the huge pipe organ in front. And the carpeting and stained glass windows. Even padded pews. Everything I saw reminded me about how different things are in Haiti.

But one thing is the same. The Bible, with its Christian message of hope. Today, all over the world, in all kinds of buildings, people are hearing about Jesus! Lord, Your Word must be special if the same verses help everybody in all the different cultures! Like, wow!

The minister started to read Matthew 10:29-31:
"Are not two sparrows sold for a penny? Yet not one of them will fall to the ground apart from the will of your Father. And even the very hairs of your head are all numbered. So don't be afraid; you are worth more than many sparrows."

The point of the sermon was that each one of us is valuable. Well, actually, according to the minister, there were *three* points. But I can't remember the other two. Lord, how come there are always three points?

When the ushers collect the offering, I usually concentrate very hard on not dropping the plate! But this time I

44

looked at all the money and checks, and I realized that some of the offering goes to help people in other countries like Haiti.

Well, on the way home, Mom actually said something about the sermon! It's the first time. "I realized I'm a bird snob," she said.

"What do you mean?" Dad asked.

"Now that I'm getting better at identifying birds at our feeder, I get excited only about the special ones," Mom explained. "And I get most excited about a new one that I've never seen before. I don't even watch the sparrows on the ground."

"Don't they eat at the feeder?" Pete asked.

"No," Mom said. "They just sort of hang around underneath and eat what the other birds drop."

"So," I said, "the point of the sermon is that God cares just as much about ordinary people."

"What's that got to do with birds?" Justin asked. He's never been good at analogies.

Dad explained. "The rest of the verse said we are more valuable than birds."

"Well, who doesn't know that?" Justin said. "Big deal!"

"The Lord knows everything about us," Mom said. "Even how many hairs we have on our heads!"

"Does he know about Pete's haircut?" Justin asked.

At first, the car was quiet. Then Pete looked right at Justin and yelled, "Drop dead, you little creep!" He hasn't said that in months.

"That's enough," Dad said sternly. And we rode in silence the rest of the way home.

Lord, I'm curious. When other families discuss the sermon, is this how it is with them?

One thing, for sure. Pete did not seem very happy. He went straight to his room after we got home. Mom went into the family room and sat looking out at the birds. Dad headed for his leather chair and the fat Sunday newspaper.

I motioned to Justin to come up to my room. He shook his head. Whatever had happened, he wasn't telling.

"I'll get it," I said. I picked up the phone.

"It's Chris," she said. "Welcome home!"

"Thanks," I said. "How's Star?"

"I think he misses you. Aren't you going to ask how I am?" Chris said.

"I'm sorry. How *are* you, Chris?"

"Much better," she replied.

I wondered what she meant by that? Maybe her mom's drinking problem has improved. "Super!" I said. "Are you going out to Twin Pines this afternoon?"

"Sure am!" she said. "That's one reason I'm calling. Are you?"

"To be honest, I'm planning on it," I said. "But I still have to ask my parents. Just a sec."

I've never been super at hiding my feelings. So, naturally, Dad knew how anxious I was to see Star. Still, he teased me. "Can I come along?" he asked. "Remember, you still owe me a Christmas present!"

"That's right," I said. My gifts to the family this year were promises to spend time with or for each person. Dad is the only one who hasn't collected on his "time certificate."

"I'm just kidding about today," he said. "Do you need a ride?"

Back on the phone, I told Chris I'd meet her in an hour. Dad would drive me over, and Felix would bring me home. As the McKenna's chauffeur, he had to pick Chris up anyhow.

On my way up to my room, I detoured back into the living room. "Have you decided what you want me to do for your gift?" I asked my father.

"As a matter of fact, I have, Jennifer," he smiled. "I've been thinking that I hardly ever get to see you alone any more. Any chance you'd accept a date with a good-looking, middle-aged man?"

"I never go out with strangers," I teased.

"I promise not to be strange," Dad laughed. "How about Tuesday night? Pizza?"

"Sounds great!" I said. Climbing the stairs to my room, I felt fantastic!

I was just putting on my riding clothes when I heard the doorbell. Nobody ever rings the doorbell on Sunday afternoons.

"Jennifer," Mom called.

I couldn't believe it. Maybe it was Matthew. I rushed like mad.

There, standing in our entryway, was a guy I've never

seen before. He was holding my suitcase. "Jennifer Green?" he asked.

"Oh, thank you!" I said. "Do you always bring lost suitcases right to people's houses?"

"We do if they have names and addresses on them," he explained. "I have several others in the car."

"Thanks again," I said, closing the door after him.

Back in my room, as I unpacked, I saw that nothing was missing. However, things weren't quite the way I had packed them. Because I had traveled from another country, my suitcase had to go through customs without me!

Well, as I unpacked, I assembled my Haitian souvenirs and gifts on my dresser. I'd give them to people later. Mom was calling us to lunch.

On the way, I threw my dirty clothes down the chute. For the first time, I realized how incredible it was to toss them down to the laundry! Presto! They'd be clean and dry. Naturally, Mom had to stick them in the washer and drier. But mothers need something to do. Don't they? Suddenly, I wasn't so sure.

Pete, now dressed in regular jeans and sweat shirt, ate his sandwich without saying a word. He looked like he didn't have a friend in the world.

"OK if I go to Keever's?" Justin asked.

"Fine," Dad said. "I can drop you off on the way to the stable."

"Hey, Pete," I said. "Want to come to Twin Pines with me?" I couldn't believe I was inviting him! But, sure enough, I was!

48

Pete looked up. "Do you really want me?" he asked.

"Sure," I heard my voice say. "It'll just be Chris and me, and you two have always enjoyed each other. How about it?"

"I'd like that," my brother said. "Excuse me, please, so I can get ready."

Dad smiled at me. Mom looked like she might faint!

Chapter 7

Surprise at Twin Pines

Lord, it's me, Jennifer.

"I won't bug you," Pete told me after Dad dropped us off at Twin Pines stable. "I just need to be alone."

"You could have found a warmer place for that," I said. I mean, it's one thing if you're working up a sweat riding, but otherwise, it's freezing. Like a lumberyard in winter.

"I'll be OK," my brother said. "As a matter of fact, don't even tell Chris I'm here."

"You're kidding!" I said. "That's weird. What happens in an hour or so? Or when it's time to go home?"

"OK," he said. "Tell her if you want to. I'm going back to find an empty stall. See you later, *Jennifer.*" He emphasized my name.

Well, if my brother wanted privacy, he'd have privacy.

I hurried over to Star's stall. At first I just looked at him. My dream-come-true. He had heard me coming and edged over to where I could nuzzle his head. "Star of Wonder," I said, patting the white spot between his eyes. He felt warm.

"Have you missed me?" I asked. Naturally, he didn't say anything. But I just knew he had. Missed me, that is. After climbing down beside him, I gave him several more strokes. Then I lifted the saddle down from the hook.

"Hello!" It was Chris. I couldn't see her, but I'd know her voice anywhere.

"Hi," I yelled. "I'm with Star. Come on over!"

She was smiling and relaxed. "Has he changed? Does he look the way you remembered him?"

"I've only been gone a week!" I reminded her. "Are you going to ride too?"

"I sure am!" she said. "No lessons on Sunday! I'll get Hoagie and meet you in the ring."

"Here we go, Star! Let's really shine," I said softly, as I mounted.

Riding a horse is kind of like riding a bicycle. You don't forget how. Since Star and I were alone in the ring, we started with manege exercises. That just means riding around in special patterns—like on a huge game board.

We changed gaits smoothly. "Super!" I said. It was as if I hadn't even been gone.

"Looking good," Chris smiled. I watched her mount Hoagie. I used to think you had to watch your own horse, but that was before I learned to ride by *feel*.

Remembering back to my first lessons, I realized again what a good teacher Chris had been.

"It feels excellent!" I was getting hot. Suddenly, I remembered Pete and wondered where he was.

Mostly, we didn't talk. Chris and I, that is. I couldn't hear what she said to her horse. And what I say to Star is pretty private.

Finally, I pulled up near the gate and watched Chris and Hoagie. No wonder she wins all those ribbons at horse shows! They're hung all around her room, near the ceiling, and mostly they're blue. You know what that means!

"Hi, Pete!" Chris smiled and waved. I turned around.

"Hi, Chris!" Pete, grinning from ear to ear, waved back. He was acting totally normal. None of that *cool* stuff. Personally, I think he's had his eye on Chris since the first time I invited her over for dinner. But that's really dumb, since he's two years younger.

Oddly enough, Chris seems to enjoy Pete too. Probably she thinks of him as the little brother she doesn't have. Being an only child must be really lonely. Especially with a mother like Mrs. McKenna—one who gets drunk. I'm the only one Chris has told about that, and for once, I've kept my big mouth shut.

Pete and I watched Chris put some rails in the center of the ring. It was the first time I had ever seen her jump! Frankly, it surprised me that she decided to do it today.

But Pete was a better audience. He took off his gloves and clapped, stamped his feet, and cheered. Maybe he was just cold. Surely he didn't think Chris was trying to impress *him!*

I'd had enough. I signaled to Star that our rest was over. Then I cantered around the ring toward the right. Chris and Hoagie followed us. I could hear them.

"Let's reverse," Chris said.

I grinned. Now Star and I were the ones following. Chris began a slow trot, and I did it too. It was like playing tag. I was having so much fun, I forgot all about Pete. This was the most fun I'd had in ages.

Suddenly, Chris cut in and rode toward the rails. I couldn't believe it. She knows I'm just starting to jump! I pulled up my reins and watched her gracefully clear the hurdle. Now why would she do that? Was she trying to prove she is a better rider than I am? Was she showing off—to Pete?!

"Super!" yelled Pete, going into his excited applause routine.

Breathless, Chris turned to me. "Time out?" she asked.

"I guess so," I said. We both dismounted. Frankly, that just means we got off.

When Star and I turned toward his stall, Pete followed Chris.

"I can't believe it!" I said to Star. I brushed and wiped him down before I gave him his carrot. If I listened carefully, I could hear Pete and Chris talking.

Later, the three of us were sitting near the door waiting for Felix. "How was Haiti?" Chris asked.

"I wish you could go and see everything," I said. "Hey! Any chance you could?"

"Probably," Chris said. "I've never thought about it before. Are you going again?"

"I'd like to," I said.

"Hey," Pete complained. "How about my turn?"

He had a point. But now I have a special reason for wanting to go back. Her name is Kirlene, and she's my own sponsored girl.

"Maybe sometime Grandma would take all of us," I said slowly. "While we were there, she picked out another child to sponsor—a boy," I told them. "Grandma already sponsors a girl. We met her last week!"

"What's *sponsor?*" Chris asked.

"You send money every month to help a particular child," I explained. "As a matter of fact, I have a girl myself!"

"You do?" Pete was surprised.

"Well, I picked out her picture just before I left Haiti. So we haven't met. And we haven't had time to write to each other yet," I said.

"Where are you getting the money?" Pete was suspicious.

"That's a problem," I admitted. "I have to think of a way. Any ideas?"

"You could muck stables," Chris said right away.

"Yuck!" said Pete.

"How much does it pay?" I asked.

Chris told me. "Lots of people don't want to do it. But

there are people here who are looking for help. I can't clean any more than I'm doing now."

"It's a perfect solution!" I said. "Chris you're terrific!"

"I agree!" Pete agreed.

"So what else is new?" She smiled. At the stables, she's always very confident. But, to be honest, I think she's insecure around kids our age.

"Can you get me the names of some customers?" I asked. "And," I grinned, "can you show me how?"

"Yuck!" said Pete again.

"Shut up," I told him. But he could see I was smiling.

At that point, Felix drove up and waved. I got in first, followed by Chris, and then Pete. He actually held the door open for us.

"Can you come home with us?" Pete asked Chris.

"You mean now?"

"Why not?" he asked.

"I have youth group," I reminded him.

"Well, I don't," Pete reminded me. "How about it, Chris? We could play ping pong."

"I need a shower," she told him.

"You could take one at our house," Pete said. "And you and Jennifer are about the same size." He looked across Chris at me. "Couldn't you lend her something?"

"Well, sure," I said. He hadn't even asked permission. "Are Mom and Dad going to be home?"

"I'd love to come, Pete, but I'd better not," Chris interrupted. "This time would be too complicated."

56

At least *she* was showing some good judgment. As for Pete, I felt more confused than when he was acting weird. But I didn't say anything then to either of them.

"So," I broke the silence. "How's Nellie?" She's Felix's wife and the cook at McKennas'.

"Her back's bad," Felix said.

"Tell her I hope she feels better soon," I said.

We pulled into our lane, and Pete jumped out of the car and ran around to open my door. I nearly fainted.

"Thanks, Felix," I said. "See you tomorrow?" I asked Chris.

"Tomorrow," she smiled. "Right after school. How about a jumping lesson?"

"Great!" I said. "And maybe you could show me the right way to clean a stable."

Chris laughed. "Right!"

"Yuck!" Pete said. Very original. "Bye, Chris."

"Good-bye, Pete. See ya."

"Yeah." They smiled at each other. I couldn't believe it.

We waved at Chris, then went in the front door. I'd have to hurry to shower before youth group.

Chapter 8

Will Everyone Who's Insecure Please Stand Up!

Lord, it's me, Jennifer.

As You know, I rode to youth group with Harringtons. Mrs. H. drove, Matthew sat in the front seat next to her, and I was in the back with Mack. It was pretty boring. Mrs. Harrington did most of the talking.

Our meeting consisted of a Bible relay. Frankly, if I had known that in advance, I just might have stayed home. Nothing personal, You know. But things like that still make me very nervous. It's like being forced to run a race with a broken leg and having to pretend nothing's wrong. I hate faking it. Maybe I should memorize the books of the Bible.

"I Peter 3:9," Mr. Anderson called out.

Boy, was I relieved! At least I knew it was in the New

Testament! I fumbled past the four Gospels. Suddenly, I found myself in Peter!

I ran my finger down the page, jumped up, and started reading: "The Lord is not slow in keeping his promise, as some understand slowness. He is patient with you, not wanting anyone to perish, but everyone to come to repentance."

Well, naturally You know what happened. I had goofed. Peter wrote *two* different Peters, and the verse I read is in the second one.

"Someone on the other team?" Mr. Anderson said.

Kelly stood up and read in a clear voice: "Do not repay evil with evil or insult with insult, but with blessing, because to this you were called so that you may inherit a blessing."

"It could happen to anyone," Heidi said later.

"But I feel so stupid," I groaned.

"Forget it," my friend comforted. "They're both useful things to remember!" Naturally, Heidi was right. But why did I feel so crummy?

During refreshments, Mr. Anderson read the list of committee members for our February social. Matthew is on the committee with Heidi, Kelly, Rebecca Carlson, and some other kids. It was Matthew's idea to meet right away in the corner of the room. So Heidi excused herself and headed over.

"We've had some good socials this year!" Mack said as he sat down in the seat Heidi had left. "Especially ours!"

I laughed. And, like magic, I forgot about my goof-up

and started feeling sensational. "I agree," I said. "The Christmas party was awesome."

"And don't forget the hayride!" Mack said.

As if I ever could! "Right!" I agreed. I hoped I wasn't blushing. That was my first "date" with Matthew. The time he held my hand on the hay wagon. I'm sure You remember!

"Wonder what they'll come up with for February?" Mack reached over and took my cup. He smiled. "Want some more cocoa?"

Well, we didn't have to wait long to find out about the February party. "It's going to be a Valentine Party!" Heidi told us.

"All right!" Mack approved. "More cocoa, Heidi?" He smiled, reached over, and took her cup.

After youth group, lots of the kids stay for church. But I felt pooped. I decided to call home. "Can somebody pick me up?" I asked Mom.

As soon as I got in the car, Mom wanted to know if I was OK. She felt my forehead like she always does. "You feel warm." I'm sure she regards this system as accurate as a thermometer. Maybe even more accurate.

"I'm beat!" I told her.

"Well, you've had an exciting week and a long day," she reminded me.

Well, whatever. I went straight up to my room, pulled down the shades, and put on my pajamas. I crawled into bed without taking my bedspread off. Which is against the rules. *So ground me!* I thought.

And the next thing I knew, it was morning. I realized I hadn't even brushed my teeth. Yuck! Still, I realized I wasn't sick. Mom had been right. When you add in the trip to Haiti, it had been quite a Christmas holiday!

It was hard to believe I had to go back to school today. Talk about culture shock! On the other hand, I remembered how few of the Haitian kids have the opportunity to go to school. That helped me get my act together.

Since my bus leaves earlier than my brothers', I usually don't even see them in the morning. But Pete was already up and creating an uproar in the kitchen.

"I really can't see how that outfit is going to improve your popularity!" Mom was telling him.

I was inclined to agree. I guess some people can pull it off, but to accept Pete as a punk rock type was stretching the imagination a bit too far. But I didn't say so.

"You'll see," Pete defended himself. "Scott and I are going to be the coolest dudes in the school."

"Just how," Mom asked, "are you going to wear your ski cap with your hair sticking up like that?"

Pete adjusted his sunglasses. "Aw Mom," he said, "have you ever seen a cool dude wearing a ski hat? Come on!"

Well, You probably witnessed the whole scene. Personally, I had to get to the corner or I'd miss my bus.

"Has Keever been going through anything weird lately?" I asked Heidi on the bus.

"Huh uh," Heidi said. "He did mention trying out for a school play. Why? Has Justin?"

"Not Justin," I said. "But you wouldn't believe the way Pete looks this morning."

Heidi laughed. "We saw him yesterday. What's going on?"

"I'm not sure," I told her. "I think the kids at school are teasing him about going to Sunday school. But don't say anything."

"I won't. Can't he handle it?"

"Personally, I think he's really insecure," I said.

"So, who isn't?" Heidi said.

"You mean, you think everybody is?" I asked. "Insecure, that is?"

"Probably, if they were honest. Aren't you?"

"It's getting better," I admitted. "Having friends helps a lot."

"I agree. Isn't Pete in sixth grade? Sixth grade is hard. I can remember thinking I was the only person in the world who didn't fit in," Heidi said.

"What did you do?" I wondered.

"Mom said just to be myself," Heidi said.

"It worked out great for you," I admitted.

"Partly with your help, Jennifer." We smiled at each other. That whole thing was another story.

"Do you think that would make Pete popular?" I asked. "Just being himself? Does that work for everybody?"

"I'm not sure," Heidi admitted.

"What's the serious conversation about?" Matthew asked as he and Mack passed us on their way off the bus.

We hadn't even realized we were already at school!

* * * * * * * *

During the day, I was surprised at how easily I slipped back into my school routine. We were starting new units in social studies and math. Stuff like that. Naturally, my next theme for English would be on Haiti. But all in all, school seemed about the same as it was before vacation. Pretty boring.

After my last class, instead of taking my regular bus home, I took the route that goes near Twin Pines. That way, Mom doesn't always have to drive me. Chris was already there.

"I'll be ready in a sec," I told her.

Chris sat on the rail and watched me enter the ring. "Before we get into the jumping, I think we should brush up on some schooling movements," she told me.

Although I felt a little disappointed, I had to admit it probably was a good idea. I had been gone the whole week before, and I haven't gotten much riding time in ever since Dad bought Star for me. Life is always hectic before Christmas.

"OK, Star," I said softly, "now it's *your* turn for school!" And *mine* too, I had to admit. We are a team. And every team has to learn to work together.

"Start with some trotting and stopping," Chris told us.

I trotted a third of the way around the ring. With my eyes up, I closed my hands on the reins, holding the pressure until Star stopped. I relaxed my hands and counted to five. Then we started forward again, going from a walk to a slow trot to a posting trot.

"Be sure he stops in a straight line," Chris called. "Don't let him swing his hindquarters into the ring!"

When Star stops, he really stops. Some horses move around or turn. Someone had trained him well.

"While you stand still, you can stroke him," Chris suggested. I was stopped right in front of her. "It might not relax Star, but it will relax you!" Chris explained.

Star and I went on to do the *circle* and the *figure eight*. Finally, we got to practice a few "jumps." I mean, any horse could have easily walked over that pole on the ground, but it represented something higher. I knew it, and so did Star.

* * * * * * * *

"Nothing to it!" Chris laughed, as she demonstrated how to clean out a stall.

"Did you get the names of anyone who needs my services?" I asked.

She handed me a piece of paper. "Call these," she suggested.

"Thanks." I put the two names in my pocket.

"So long, dear Star," I said, giving my horse one last pat. "See you tomorrow!"

"Who's picking you up?" Chris wondered.

"Dad," I said. "On his way home from work."

"Is there anything wrong?" she asked.

Chris must be the most sensitive person in the whole world. How could she tell? That's what I want to know. "What do you mean?" I said.

"You've been acting different today."

Well, there was no use faking it. "I was surprised yesterday when you showed off in front of Pete," I said. "It looked like you were making a play for him."

"Oh, that."

"Yes, that."

"He seems to like me," Chris said slowly.

"He always has," I told her.

"Not this way. He's a lot more mature lately."

"Confidentially, he's very insecure right now," I told her. "It's stupid to hurt him," I said.

"Who's hurting him?" Chris asked. "Did it ever occur to you that I just might like him too?"

"But he's only in sixth grade," I protested.

"So? He's taller than we are," Chris said. "Have you seen many other guys giving me any attention? Well, for your information, they don't." Her lip quivered. "As a matter of fact, I'm pretty insecure myself right now. Maybe you've been so busy having fun yourself that you haven't noticed."

I just looked at her. "Oh, my goodness," I said, as Dad drove up. "I'm sorry, Chris."

"See ya tomorrow," she said.

Chapter 9

Pete's Next Approach

Lord, it's me, Jennifer.

Pete's door was closed as I passed. I had a sudden impulse to knock.

"Who is it?" my brother asked.

"Jennifer."

Pause. "Come in."

He was sitting on his bed, reading. That figured. His shades lay on the bedspread.

"How was your day?" I asked.

"Cool," he said. But he had changed his clothes. He looked a lot different than he had this morning. "Promise you won't laugh."

"Promise."

"Scott freaked everybody out," he said.

"And you?"

He took a deep breath. "They laughed. I was so embarrassed I'd have left school if I could."

"Maybe it was too much change all at once," I suggested. "They didn't have time to get used to it."

"Frankly, I don't think it suited my personality," Pete said.

"Well, that too," I agreed. "Have you considered just being yourself?"

"That's the advice I've heard all my life," Pete told me. "But *being myself* is what I've been doing all my life. And it hasn't won me any popularity contests."

"Maybe you're a late bloomer," I said. "You'll probably be voted most popular in high school."

"Forget it," my brother told me. "I can't wait that long. I need to improve myself right now!"

"Well, good luck," I said. And I meant it. But if I didn't hurry up and get my shower, I'd miss dinner.

"Thanks for caring." Pete stood up. He smiled. "And, as a matter of fact," he added, "I have a brand new approach."

I smiled as I left. Frankly, I hope it works better than the last one! By the way, Pete *is* taller than I am. I can't believe it.

* * * * * * * *

"Hi, Mom!" Pete said, as he took his place at the table. "Oh, may I help you with your chair?"

Mom looked startled. "Are you OK?"

Pete smiled. "I certainly am. How was your day?" By now everybody looked startled.

"Pretty good," Mom said. "I answered a classified ad for a part-time job."

"No kidding!" Dad looked surprised. "How come you didn't mention it?"

"I didn't notice the ad until everybody had gone. I was reading the paper, and there it was! So I got dressed up and went over for an interview."

"Did you get the job?" Justin asked.

"I don't know. They said they'd call." Mom looked excited.

We still hadn't prayed. And the food was getting cold. Finally, Dad remembered. He called on Justin. After Justin had prayed, Pete said, "How was basketball practice, Jus?" He's never been so friendly in his whole life.

"How come you want to know?" Justin was suspicious.

"Just interested," Pete said. "I hear you're the rising star of the team."

Justin looked embarrassed. "Well," he said, "I am one of the best shots from the outside. Of course, a little height would help."

"I'd give you some of mine if I could," Pete told him.

"Lay off!" Justin warned.

"I mean it," Pete continued. But he should have quit when he was ahead. Justin concentrated on eating.

"Son, your food's getting cold," Dad said.

"Right you are, Father!" Pete grinned. He picked up

his fork. "Jennifer, why don't you tell everybody about Kirlene?"

"New kid in school?" Dad asked.

"No," I said. "There are never any new kids in school. I'm still the newest." Everybody was waiting. "Kirlene's a girl in Haiti. I'm going to sponsor her."

"What does that mean?" Justin asked.

"I'm going to be sort of like a pen pal. We'll write to each other," I explained. "But the most important thing is that I'm going to send money each month to help change her world."

"Wow," Justin said.

"That sounds like a big investment," Dad said. "Did you just win a lottery?"

"No," I laughed. "I can't change the whole country! But by sending a check every month, I can change Kirlene's life. She'll get food, and clothes, and the chance to go to school, and everything."

"Is this what Grandma does?" Mom asked.

"Right," I said. "That's why we went to Haiti. We actually visited the girl she sponsors. You'll see her picture as soon as I get my film developed. And Grandma picked out another kid when we were down there—a boy. She chose him when I took Kirlene."

"Do you have a picture of Kirlene?" Mom asked.

"I do, in my room," I said. "May I please be excused to get it?"

When I passed the blue folder around, everybody looked carefully. "Isn't she beautiful?" I asked.

"Sure is!" Pete was the first to answer. "And I'll bet everybody's wondering where you're getting the money." He smiled at me. Again.

I felt shy. "I wanted this sponsoring to be my own thing," I explained. "I wasn't sure how I was going to do it, but I wanted to earn the money myself."

"And?" Dad asked.

"I'm probably going to clean out stables at Twin Pines. Chris has given me a couple names to call."

"Yuck," Justin said. I knew he would. Say it, that is.

"And I'm paying somebody to clean out Star's stall!" Dad said.

"I'll do Star's, Dad," I told him. "It should have been part of my responsibility anyhow."

"Fair enough," Dad said. "On that basis, I could advance you the money for your first month's sponsorship payment," he offered. "I'll give you a check after dinner."

I never felt so happy in my life. Did You work it out, Lord? Thanks!

* * * * * * * *

I was starting to write my theme for English when Pete knocked at my door. I knew it was him. The old five knocks, pause, and two more.

"Come on in," I said.

He was still smiling. "You're overdoing it," I told him. "Looking pleasant is one thing. But that constant grin makes you look pretty stupid."

"I suppose you're right," he said. "But are you getting the message that *I'm friendly?*"

"I'm getting the message," I said. "But you have to mean it or it doesn't count."

"I know. By the way, what do you think is my best physical feature?" he asked.

I looked at Pete again. "Beats me. Why don't you ask Justin? He's pretty sharp on styles."

"A brilliant idea!" he said. "I wonder why I didn't think of that in the first place?" And he was gone.

Well, every time I started to write about Haiti, all I could think of was Kirlene. Finally, I got out my stationary. If I wrote to her, I could sent the letter with my first monthly check.

Dear Kirlene,

My name is Jennifer Green, and I'm your new sponsor. That means I will be sending money every month so you can go to school, etc.

First of all, I want you to know that I just got home from visiting Haiti. I went with my Grandmother. She is a sponsor too. While I was there, I decided I wanted to help someone, and I picked out your picture.

You probably are wondering what I'm like. Well, I am just a normal girl. My hair is brown and I have braces on my teeth. I am enclosing one of my school pictures. Since it was taken, I got my hair cut. So you will have to imagine it shorter.

I go to a big school. I am in the eighth grade. My

favorite subject is English. I like to write. Also, I talk a lot.

As for my family, I have a mother and father and two brothers. Pete is in sixth grade, and Justin is in fourth. Justin likes sports.

You will be surprised to know that I have my own horse. His name is Star, and I got him for Christmas. When I was in Haiti, I rode a horse to the Citadelle. Have you been there?

Just in case you're wondering, I am earning the money I am sending for you. I am working in a stable. That's a place where horses are kept.

Please write when you have time. Tell me about yourself—your family, your favorite subject in school, and stuff like that. I am very interested.

I forgot to mention that I am a Christian. I hope you are one too.

> *Sincerely,*
> *Jennifer Green*

I read the letter over. Is it too long? Lord, I know I haven't started earning the money yet, but I figure I will by the time she gets this. Hope that's OK.

I looked at *Sincerely*. It sounded very official, but not particularly friendly. So I erased it and wrote *Love*. I hope that's not overdoing it at this stage in our relationship. Is it? As you know, I couldn't erase it again. So I had no choice.

After addressing the envelope, I folded the letter, and stuck in the check. Just before I licked it, I remember about my picture. It took me nearly fifteen minutes to find one. But, after all, I have hers, don't I?

Returning to my theme on Haiti, I discovered it was much easier to write. I think the reason is that now I'm personally involved. Do You agree?

I took time out to call the two numbers Chris had given me, but no one answered either one. Personally, I didn't get one single phone call. Do You think I'm losing my popularity?

Chapter 10

What's So Funny?

Lord, it's me, Jennifer.

I was coming out of the bathroom when I discovered Pete waiting to get in. "Hi," he said, "I'm Pete Green. What's your name?"

"Are you out of your mind?" I asked.

"No, just practicing," my brother said. "It's a good way to meet strangers."

"Are there a lot of strangers to meet?" I asked.

"Well, no," Pete admitted. "But at least now I'm prepared."

"Great," I said, edging toward my room.

As I slipped into my blue slacks and vest, I decided he probably was getting these brilliant ideas from some book. That's like Pete. He approaches life like a problem to be solved.

75

"Good morning," I said to Mom.

"Hi!" She was wearing jeans.

"Anything on for today?"

"Not much," she said. "I'll finish my thank-you notes and put away the rest of the Christmas stuff."

It isn't much fun to be alone. I felt sorry for her. I hope she's into boring.

"Dad said you're having supper out with him tonight."

"I nearly forgot," I said. "Yes. We've got a date to have pizza. It's what he picked for his Christmas present."

"Have fun!" Mom said. "I think I'll take the guys to McDonalds."

"Are you picking me up at Twin Pines?"

She nodded. "See you then."

As I neared the bus stop, I could see that Stephanie Cantrell and Lindsay Porterfield were already there. Although they're both in my homeroom, we've hardly talked since I got my horse. They aren't exactly my type. Or maybe it's just that I'm not exactly theirs.

"Hi," I said.

They looked up. "Hi."

Remembering Pete, I felt like saying, "My name is Jennifer Green. What's yours?" But I didn't. "Have a nice holiday?"

"Uh huh," Stephanie said. "I hear you went on a cruise."

"No, but I spent a week in Haiti," I said. "I flew down."

76

"Oh. Was it romantic?" Lindsay asked.

"What do you mean?" I stalled for time.

"You know, *romantic!* Like, meet any cute guys?"

I shook my head. "To be honest, I wasn't looking for any."

"Oh, come off it! That's what you call being honest?" Stephanie asked.

"I was with my grandmother," I explained.

"So?"

Lindsay can be a real creep. Is it my imagination, or is she getting worse? "There's a lot more to life than looking for guys," I said.

Lindsay just smiled and raised her eyebrows. This whole conversation was really dumb.

I was relieved when Stephanie changed the subject. "Jennifer, I hear your brother's hysterical," she said. "Jeff told us Pete had the whole sixth grade in stitches yesterday."

Oh, no. Poor Pete! I didn't know what to say.

"All of a sudden, Jeff really thinks Pete could be on TV," Stephanie continued. "Of course, Jeff thinks *he's* a talent scout." She smiled a friendly kind of smile.

I couldn't believe it. Pete, a comedian? "I've never really thought of him that way," I admitted. "But I guess sometimes people are different at home."

"True," Stephanie agreed. "Jeff seems to have a lot of friends, but he drives Ashlie and me up the wall." She turned to Lindsay. "See what you're missing by not having a younger brother?"

"I might find out," Lindsay said. "My father has been dating a woman with two sons."

"No kidding!" Stephanie said.

I wonder what it would be like to have my parents split up and dating other people. I can't imagine it. Not at all.

The neighborhood guys had assembled while we were talking. When the school bus approached, everybody stood back to keep from getting splattered with slush.

As usual, I sat alone, waiting for Heidi. But today was different. Ignoring the whistles and giggles from the guys in the back of the bus, Matthew sat down next to me.

"Hi," he said.

"Hi, yourself," I smiled. "What's up?"

"Not much." He smiled back, and I melted. "I just haven't had one minute to talk to you since you got back from your trip."

"What about Heidi?" I said. Everybody knows she always sits with me when we get to her stop.

"She'll cope," he said. "Got plans after school?"

"I'm going to the stables."

"Every day?" he asked.

"Well, almost," I realized.

"I never thought I'd be jealous of a horse," Matthew told me. "Will this go on forever?"

"As a matter of fact, besides riding Star, I think I'll be working. Cleaning stables," I said. "Of course, I can probably get someone to cover for me some of the time."

"It sounds like my idea of getting an after-school job wasn't such a bad one after all," Matthew said. "I've been thinking about it for quite a while. But you already know that."

"Have you decided what you'd like to do?" I asked.

"I still don't know. Most people wouldn't hire me until I'm a year older, so that limits the options," he said.

Heidi got on the bus, smiled at us, and sat down with a seventh-grade girl. We smiled back.

Matthew stretched out his long legs. "I'm thinking of trying for a job at the hardware store. Or," he glanced at me, "I still could tutor Megan. She asked me again."

I tried to act cool. Megan, the ninth-grade beauty. The girl from the Winter Carnival committee. Now it was my turn to feel jealous! Did Matthew notice?

"Actually, I think it would be quite a challenge," Matthew continued. "Megan just acts like a dim bulb to get attention. If she'd apply herself, she could get top grades. Maybe even get into a good college."

A challenge indeed! "Which subject?" I asked.

"I guess most of them," Matthew admitted.

Sure! Sweet, gullible Matthew! But I acted real cool. "What would you do at the hardware store?"

"They need someone to learn glazing. You know, cutting glass for picture framing. Stuff like that," he told me. "When my brother goes to college, they won't have anyone to do it."

"When did Mark start working there?" I asked. I felt encouraged. Having a brother already working at the hardware store would surely give Matthew a better chance.

"He's been there a couple of summers. Of course, he's so busy in sports that he hasn't had much time for working during the school year."

The bus was nearly at school. "Jennifer," Matthew smiled, "mainly I want to ask you to go with me to the game Friday night." He is so cool.

"Sounds great!" I told him. "I'll run it past my folks and let you know."

"Mack's going to ask Heidi," Matthew said. "Surprise!" He laughed, and so did I. The four of us have done stuff together pretty often.

Suddenly, as we were getting off the bus, I was aware that the guys in back had started chanting. "Jenny. Jenny. Jenny. Jenny."

"See ya, Jenny!" Matthew said. He turned toward the stairs.

I think I blushed. There wasn't any time then to discuss my name with him. *Jenny,* indeed! Frankly, I have to admit that it sounded better when Matthew said it. Better than Pete, that is!

I noticed Heidi walking with Mack. I smiled as I watched them talk. Being included feels marvelous!

* * * * * * * *

After school today, I beat Chris to the stable. I shoveled out Star's stall and put in clean hay.

"Did you mind it when I changed your name, Star?" I stroked his head with my right hand. "Which sounds

80

better, *Jennifer* or *Jenny?*" He just sniffed my pocket. The one where I keep the carrots.

Out in the ring, Star and I finished doing circles and figure eights. Then we tried the serpentine. That involves riding back and forth across the ring. Naturally, you have to keep turning at both sides. I think I need more practice than Star does! But I never get tired of riding.

"Looking good," Chris encouraged. When I noticed she had saddled Hoagie, I knew I wouldn't be having a lesson today. Sometimes Chris rides to get rid of tension. I can usually tell. So today I didn't bother her.

"Did you get the jobs?" Chris asked later, when we had both finished grooming our horses.

"I couldn't reach either number," I told her. "I'll keep trying. Are you OK?"

"I'm fine now." She smiled.

"I have another question, Chris. This might sound stupid, but have you ever thought of Pete as funny? I mean *amusing?*" I asked.

"Are you kidding?" She looked at me. "Well, obviously you're not! I think Pete's hilarious! I always have."

"Really? But he's so shy."

"Lots of famous comedians are shy," Chris told me. "That's what my father says."

"You mean they cover up their shyness with humor?" I asked.

"Sure. Lots of people do." She looked at me. Chris never beats around the bush. "Including you!"

"Me?" As You know, I'm a typical extravert—at least

in front of other people. Suddenly, I laughed. "You know, I think you might be right!"

"See!" She laughed too.

"Well, what do you know!" Lord did You know it all the time?

"There's your mom's car," Chris said. "By the way, I won't be here tomorrow. I have a meeting. But how about a lesson the next day? If we're going to get you ready for a horse show, we have to get going!"

"Me?" I yelled.

"Yes, you!" Chris smiled as I waved and raced for Mom's car.

Chapter 11

Lucky, Lucky, Lucky Me

Lord, it's me, Jennifer.

"What looks good?" Dad asked. We were sitting together in a booth in the back of the pizza parlor.

"To be honest, I'm strictly a sausage and cheese person," I told him. "Hope you aren't disappointed."

Dad laughed. "No, not disappointed. Relieved! I was afraid I was in for pepperoni, anchovies, and mushrooms. And a stomachache to match."

"Can I get you something to drink?" the waitress asked.

"Pepsi for me," Dad said. "Jennifer?"

"The same."

"Make it a pitcher," Dad told her. "We're ready to order."

It was neat sipping our drinks in the dark while we waited.

"Mom still hasn't heard about her job," I reported.

"For tonight," Dad said, "let's talk about us. Not the rest of the family. That's one reason I wanted some time with you alone. Just to catch up."

"OK," I said.

Nobody said anything. Nothing at all. I took another sip of my drink. I'd have to be careful, or it would be all gone before the pizza even arrived.

"Do you ever make New Year's resolutions?" Dad asked.

"I don't think so." I tried to think. "Do you?"

He laughed. "I should have known you'd think it was a loaded question. This year I decided to put my family ahead of my business."

"So," I asked, "is that different?"

"Well, I've always told myself that my family was my first priority," Dad said. "But somehow it's hard to keep from getting trapped into doing work that piles up at the office."

"You're home now lots more than when we lived in Illinois," I said.

"So far," Dad told me. "And I've enjoyed it, believe me! But recently my company has asked me to do more traveling from now on."

"Do you have a choice?" I asked.

"That's part of the problem. Vice presidents are expected to follow orders. The company can make it tough for a guy who won't." Dad sipped his drink.

"Why are you telling me this?" I asked.

"Just so you'll understand," he explained. "Parents don't always have easy choices."

"What does Mom think?" I asked. "And have you told Pete and Justin?"

"I haven't told the boys yet," Dad said. "But I will when I think I should. Your mom is wonderful. She says she'll support whatever I decide. Lots of women won't do that."

"That's because she loves you, I'm sure," I said. "Dad, we all do. You know that, don't you?"

"Thanks, Jennifer." He sounded very emotional.

"How about if I pray for you?" I asked.

"A great idea! I've been doing more praying myself lately."

And, speaking of praying, suddenly, the waitress delivered our pizza. I watched to see if Dad would close his eyes. He did! But I couldn't hear him saying anything out loud. So I just silently asked You to bless us. Quick, but to the point.

"How's Star?" Dad asked.

I grinned from ear to ear. "A fantasy come true!" I told him. "It's hard to explain how a person can love an animal so much!"

"I'm glad we can do this for you," he said.

"Chris says I can be in a horse show!"

"No kidding!"

"Will you come to watch me?" I asked.

"Of course!" Dad said. "I wouldn't miss it for the world."

"I'm a lucky person," I said, between bites.

"Because you have Star?"

"Well, that too, of course," I said. "But I was thinking about our family. You know, so many kids are from broken homes. Lots of people just seem to take divorce for granted. Are you and Mom different than everybody else?"

"I doubt it," Dad said.

"Would you ever get divorced?" Lord, even asking the question was scary!

"No," Dad said, without even a pause. "When we got married, your mom and I promised total commitment to each other."

"Doesn't everybody?" I asked.

"It doesn't look like it. Not these days," Dad said. "More and more people seem to forget their responsibilities and do what they think will make them happy. I just can't see it! So many families end up getting hurt."

I was glad it was pretty dark in the restaurant. I took a big breath. "Have you ever been tempted to like another woman?" I couldn't believe I was actually asking my father something so personal!

Dad smiled. "I can honestly say I never have. Not that there haven't been opportunities," he grinned. "But if a woman flirts with me, I let her know right away that I'm not interested. If you mean it, they get the message!"

"Is divorce always wrong?" I asked. "What if a man beats his wife or she is unfaithful to him?"

"Scriptures teach that God permits divorce in some

cases. But you probably know that."

I served Dad another slice of pizza and eased one onto my own plate. "Do you think it's the parents' fault that so many young couples get divorced?" I asked.

"I don't know, Jennifer," Dad said. "From what I've been hearing, many young people go into marriage as if it's something to try out. You know, see if it works. They figure they can always get divorced."

I drank some Pepsi. "How about living together?" I asked. "Then they could just split up."

"That's fairly new," Dad told me. "Openly living together never was even considered an option until quite recently. Actually, even non-religious people didn't do it. In the Bible, God warns us against it."

"Why?" I asked.

"God knows that without commitment, relationships fail and people are hurt." Dad told me. "He designed marriage for human happiness and help."

"Did Mom know that?" I asked. I remembered she hadn't gone to church.

"Probably not at first," Dad admitted. "But I hope she does now. We have lots of love and respect for each other."

"I guess I'm lucky that I've been able to see so many happy marriages," I told him.

"Having good models helps," Dad admitted. "But it doesn't guarantee that you won't make foolish mistakes yourself."

"Do you think I might?" I asked.

"I hope not," Dad said. "The Lord will guide you if you let Him. You can trust Him with your future."

"Are you sure?"

Dad smiled. "I'm sure."

"Daddy," I said, "I love you." I haven't called him that in years.

"I love you too, Jennifer. You can't imagine my joy as I watch you growing up! You're such a lovely, intelligent, caring person."

"Do you think I'm pretty?" I felt bashful.

"You are beautiful!" Dad said. "Of course, *I've* thought so since the day you were born!"

"Dad, that's just prejudice," I laughed. "I mean really?"

"I do mean really," he said. "You're pretty inside and outside."

"I've been thinking of going to college to study journalism," I told him. "What do you think?"

"It pleases me and makes me feel proud." He smiled again. "Of course, I know you might change your mind. You're still young. But a good education really means a lot in today's world. There are more and more opportunities for women."

"But maybe I'll get married," I told him.

"There's no reason why you can't do both!" he said. "Women don't have to choose. Especially in eighth grade!"

I giggled. "I really am lucky you're my father!"

"If you keep repeating it, I may take you out for another pizza next week," he laughed.

"You should hear the kids at school talk about their parents," I said. "They blame their parents for everything imaginable!"

"That's part of growing up, I guess," Dad said. "It's part of becoming independent. But a really mature person realizes that most parents just do the best they can. Unfortunately, no one ever has a parent who's perfect!"

"I think you're great!" I told him. "Well, most of the time."

Dad just laughed.

"How about Pops?"

"Your grandfather would have been the first to admit he wasn't perfect," Dad said. "However, it took me a while to stop blaming him for everything that happened to me."

"Only Jesus was perfect," I remembered. "That's what I realized on the retreat last fall."

"Do I look like Jesus?" Dad kidded.

"Well, no," I admitted. "Have you considered trying a beard?"

The waitress gave Dad the check. "Was everything all right?" she asked. Dad told her everything was fine, and we stood up. He helped me on with my coat. "To be honest, I think this was more of a present for me than for you!" I said.

"I don't think so," he told me. "I really want to know you. And it pleases me that you still listen to my ideas. That's very special. So, you see, I'm lucky too!"

On the way home we sang together. You know, oldies Dad knows, like "By the Light of the Silvery Moon." The snow looked clean in the bright moonlight. It wasn't exactly romantic, Lord, but it sure was nice.

Back in my room, I realized again how lucky I am. When I call You "Father," it really means something special! My point is, I have a great dad *plus* a loving Heavenly Father! Will You please help the kids who aren't as fortunate?

Chapter 12

Pete's Threads, Part II

Lord, it's me, Jennifer.

Mom's car was gone.

"Any idea where she is?" Dad asked.

"She said she was taking the boys to McDonald's," I told him.

Well, it wasn't a big deal. Especially once the phone started ringing. Heidi wanted to talk over what we'd wear to the basketball game. Matthew was checking to see if I could go. (Dad said I could, "But check with Mom.")

"I'll be in the study," Dad said. "I brought some work home. Thanks for going with me."

I gave him a hug. "Thank *you*," I told him. At supper, even while we were talking, I realized that not many girls could talk with their fathers like I did.

On the way up to my room, I remembered the names

Chris had given me. The people interested in somebody to clean their stables. If I really was going to sponsor Kirlene in Haiti, I had to get some customers.

I lucked out right off. The first call turned out to be a man who said my rate was cheaper than what he has been paying. However, he explained that he had paid in advance through this week. "I'll be happy to start next week," I told him. I wrote down the location of his stall and the name of his horse, Patent. "Does the name have something to do with leather?" I asked.

He laughed real hard. "No," he told me. "I'm an attorney." I didn't really get the point, but I faked it and laughed anyway.

The second person turned out to be a woman hair stylist named Meg. "You're an answer to prayer," she said. I nearly fainted. Well, it turned out that her stall is right next to Star's! And I've never even seen her because she rides when I'm at school. Meg also wants me to start next week.

"I'm in the stall-cleaning business!" I poked my head into the study and interrupted Dad. "Two calls, two customers!"

"Maybe you should considering going into sales," Dad said. "I don't usually do that well!"

Just then the garage door went up. It is easy to hear it, because the garage is right next to Dad's den.

Mom, looking exhausted, entered first. "Hi," she gasped.

"What happened?" Dad asked. "Car trouble?"

"Worse!" She collapsed on the couch. "This is positively the last time I'm ever taking your sons shopping! From now on, you can do it."

Enter Pete and Justin. They both carried bags and boxes, and neither of them looked tired at all. That figured.

"Hi!" Pete said. He positively glowed. "Wait til you get a look at my new image!"

"You got some more new clothes?" I asked.

"Cool, man!" Justin reached up and gave Pete a pat on the back.

"You gonna show us?" I asked.

"Not tonight," Pete said. "I have to work on my oral report for science."

"Which reminds me," I realized. "I have to finish my theme!"

"I've got math," Justin admitted. I couldn't believe it. As I left, I heard Mom groan.

"That bad?" Dad asked.

"That bad!" Mom said. "He tried on everything in the store at least three times."

* * * * * * * *

Although it was still dark, I could hear my brothers yelling over the drone of a hair dryer. My alarm hadn't even gone off. Lying there trying to rest was pointless. My headboard backs up to the family bathroom, and I could hear every word.

"Hold the brush in your other hand."

"I tried that already," Pete said. "Show me again."

"You'll have to bend down. I can't reach it right."

This is the last straw. When Justin started blow-drying *his* hair, it added fifteen minutes to my morning schedule. And now Pete! Give me a break!

I turned on my light and noticed my devotion book. I hadn't read it since I got home, and my bookmark was lost. I sort of flipped through the pages until I saw one called "Brothers and Sisters."

The Bible verse was from Psalm 133:1. "How good and pleasant it is when brothers live together in unity!"

True, I thought. And how rare! I smiled at the funny poem in the beginning. And then I considered the questions:

Are your family times fun? Not too bad, Lord, I have to admit. At least they're better than they used to be, don't You think?

If they are, what makes them that way? Hmmmm. I think Dad's good sense of humor is catching. Also, it's more fun when we laugh together and not "at" someone. And when we all have turns talking. And when we listen to each other.

In case they aren't, can you figure out why? That's easy. When we kids act bored, everybody knows we'd much rather be doing something else with somebody else. And I am guilty! At least, sometimes.

Is there anything you can do to help? I just admitted it, Lord. Also, I could stop putting people down. And I could listen better. As You know, I'd much rather talk!

Why does God describe Christianity in terms of family? Is it because people live in families? But some don't! Or is it because Christianity involves relationships? Christians love You, Lord, and they love other people. Am I right?

Does this tell you something? Naturally, it does. I can practice my Christianity right at home! I should have known You'd be practical!

My response is supposed to be a prayer, so here goes. Lord, help me be a good Christian at home. Help me to get along with my brothers. And my parents. Thank You that our dad loves us. And please help the kids whose fathers *don't* show them what You're like. Amen.*

My brothers were still in the bathroom. Lord, maybe You could say something to *them!* If they don't hurry, I'll miss my bus.

"I think it's the haircut," Justin hollered. "You'd better ask Mom to take you to a stylist."

"She'll never take me anywhere again. Not after last night," Pete said.

"You've got to try. It's your only hope," Justin yelled. Pete had turned off the blow dryer.

I heard the bathroom door open. Finally. But all I saw was two backs, one tall, one short, walking toward their rooms.

---

*From *Time Out for God!* by Jane Sorenson. Copyright 1986 by The Standard Publishing Company. Used by permission.

Surprisingly, it wasn't too late. The boys must have set their alarms real early. Were they considerate, Lord, or did they think I'd be mad at them?

As usual, Mom was in the kitchen. "Do you think you'll hear today?" I asked her. "About the job, I mean?"

She still looked tired. "Could be." She poured herself another cup of coffee.

"What happened last night?" I asked.

"When we finished our hamburgers, Justin offered to help Pete pick out some new clothes," she said.

"But he just got some," I remembered.

"You saw those yourself. Frankly, I was happy enough to see an end to that particular image!"

"So? What happened?"

"I drove them to the mall. But between the two of them, I thought I'd never live through the experience." She had a pained look on her face. "Justin has this incredible sense of style. And Pete won't settle for anything that isn't comfortable."

I was beginning to get the picture. Things like that do take time. And patience.

"Ta dah!" The boys came down together. Justin looked proud. Pete looked embarrassed.

"Cool!" I said. "Really awesome, Pete!"

Pete's face got red. "Do you really think so?"

Justin interrupted. "Of course, you have to imagine that his hair isn't sticking out like that!" He looked right at Mom. "Any chance you could take him for a good styling? Like today? Please?" he begged.

"I can try," Mom said. She smiled. "You do look good, Son," she told Pete.

"Thanks. You're really a patient person, you know." He sat down carefully and placed his napkin on his lap. "I'm supposed to compliment people and eat properly and have good manners."

"Good grief!" I said. "How do you remember everything?"

"Nobody said popularity is easy," Pete told me.

True. How true!

I thought about it as I ran for the bus.

Chapter 13

Growing Pains

Lord, it's me, Jennifer.

You'll probably think this is stupid. But today I realized that my brothers are growing up too! See, I was so involved in my own life that I just kept thinking of Pete and Justin as little kids. Sort of in one breath—*my little brothers.*

Frankly, to think of Pete's being in junior high next year still blows my mind! But I might as well get used to it. He definitely is not a little boy any longer!

When Mom picked me up at Twin Pines stables, the first thing she said was, "I didn't get it."

"Pete's hair appointment?" I asked.

"No," she said. "I got that. But I didn't get the job! I've never felt so rejected in my life!"

"I'm sorry," I told her. And I really was. "It's probably a stupid company. They don't deserve to have you."

"It probably wasn't very challenging work," Mom admitted. "But it would have been a start. It's been so long since I've done anything but cook and chauffeur that I don't have much confidence."

"Maybe something better will turn up," I told her. "Don't give up hope. Besides, weren't you thinking of going back to school?"

"Right," she said. "Maybe I'll do that. If only I didn't have to take tests."

"You don't like tests?"

"Even thinking about them scares me to death!" she said. She pushed the button on the garage opener.

As we pulled in, I noticed a light in Pete's room.

"I'll be down to help as soon as I shower," I told Mom.

Pete's door was open. "Hi, Jennifer!" He wore a big smile. And awesome hair! It was sort of layered and shaped, and it flipped under near his ears. Well, You probably know what a good haircut looks like.

"Pete, the lady killer!" I kidded. "Now you'll have all the girls liking you."

"Are you kidding or being honest?" he asked.

"Well, I'm teasing you, but it's probably true," I said. "Actually, most girls will hide the fact that they like you—they'll act cool. But it's only a matter of time!"

"Somebody whistled when I walked into homeroom today," Pete whispered.

"What did you do?"

"I just smiled," he grinned. "It's getting easier."

"Good," I said. "I do like your haircut!'

I dropped off my books in my room and headed for the shower.

* * * * * * * *

"Now, that's more like it!" Justin told Pete as we sat down to supper. He nodded approval, then turned to Mom. "Where's Dad?"

"He had to go to Boston," she said.

"Justin, may I please have some butter?" Pete said.

"Here," Justin shoved it over.

"Thank you very much," Pete replied.

"What's wrong with you?" Justin asked.

"Can't a person be polite? I'm practicing my manners." Pete was serious. "Good manners are important in being popular."

"Says who?" Justin wanted to know.

"My book on popularity," Pete explained. "It says girls should be cool, friendly but not pushy. And boys should have good manners."

Justin acted surprised. "Is that right, Jennifer?"

Well, I'm not used to being asked for advice. Particularly by my brothers! "It sounds pretty good to me," I said.

"See?" Pete said.

"See?" Mom smiled. "You mean everything I've tried to teach you hasn't been wasted?"

"Mom, I meant to compliment you on the casserole," Pete said.

"Do you need another favor?" Mom was suspicious.

"No thank you, Mom. I just need the salt."

"This is getting sickening," Justin groaned.

We ate in silence for a few minutes. Frankly, it was a relief. We aren't used to acting this good. Especially with Dad gone.

"How was basketball practice, Jus?" Pete was at it again. "Do you have a game coming up?"

"It was OK."

"Justin, you're lucky to have something to do after school," Pete said. "I think that's the hardest thing about not being a jock. There's not much to do after school."

Personally, I always thought having the kids tease him was the hardest thing. But he isn't going to admit that at dinner. Right?

I decided to change the subject. "I'm starting to get ready to enter a horse show," I said. "I'm feeling more and more confident with Star."

"How's Chris?" Pete asked.

"Fine. Why?"

"Just curious," Pete said. "Can't I even ask?"

I had visions of him asking her for a date, and I nearly choked.

"Jennifer, you certainly look pretty in blue," Pete said.

"Thanks, but what's going on with you?"

"More popularity," Justin said. "He's probably supposed to say something nice about everybody. I'll bet it's my turn next!"

"Was it that obvious?" Pete asked.

"I'm afraid so," Mom told him.

"People will think you want to borrow something," Justin said.

Pete looked discouraged. "In the book, one of the suggestions is *I admire your posture.* But nobody's sitting up straight!"

We all roared. "I can't believe it!" I giggled.

"I give up," Pete said. "What's the use?"

"We aren't laughing *at* you, Pete," I told him. "In the popularity book, what was the *point* of complimenting people?"

"You won't laugh?" he asked.

"Promise!" I said. "Actually, we all can probably learn something. Right, Justin?"

"Right," he said. I was afraid he'd start laughing again, but he managed not to. Laugh, that is.

"OK," Pete explained. "The point is that if you make people feel good, they'll want to have you around. You're supposed to spread joy by complimenting people. Also," he added, "it says people like it if you use their names a lot."

"But there's more to conversation than that," Mom told him.

"I know, Mom, but I haven't gotten to that part yet." This time he laughed with us.

"Keep us posted," I giggled.

"You'll probably be able to guess," Pete said. He probably was right. "By the way, have you heard any good jokes lately?"

"Is that in the book?" Mom asked.

"No."

"Then why are you asking?" I wondered.

"Can't a person learn a few jokes without his family making it into a big deal?" Pete asked.

At first, nobody said anything. To be honest, I hadn't heard a joke in ages, and I said so.

"How long will Dad be gone?" Justin asked.

"He wasn't sure," Mom said.

* * * * * * * *

While I was copying over my theme, Heidi called. We decided to wear skirts to the basketball game instead of pants. Personally, I think it's because she just got a new skirt for Christmas.

Next, I got a call from Matthew saying he had an appointment with the owner of the hardware store. Although I felt like cheering, I played it cool. Boo, Megan!

I also got a call from Chris saying that there's an announcement about horse shows in the new horse magazine. I told her my copy hadn't come yet.

My brothers got one phone call each. (I could tell, because I heard Mom call them.)

I stacked my homework in a pile and went downstairs. Mom was reading in the family room. "Good night." I kissed her. "Lonely?"

"Sort of," she said. "I've gotten used to telling your father everything at the end of the day. I miss that."

"Didn't he call?"

"Yes," she said. "but it isn't the same."

"See you in the morning."

"Thanks for coming down," Mom said.

Pete's door was still open. "Still studying popularity?" I asked. He had books all over his room.

"No time tonight for popularity," Pete said. "I'm giving a report on bumblebees. Did you know that the word bumblebee comes from the Middle English word *bumblen,* which means *humming?"*

"No, Pete," I said, "I didn't know that."

"What's 'Middle English?'"

"I have no idea. We haven't studied that yet," I said. "By the way, what goes zzub, zzub, zzub?"

"I give up."

"A bee flying backwards," I said.

"Hey! Maybe I can work that into my talk."

I groaned. "You wouldn't!"

"Try me," he said, grinning. "What do you get if you cross a stereo and a refrigerator?"

"Beats me!" I said.

"Very cool music! Get it?"

Well, naturally I did. I tried to think of one. "How do you get down from an elephant?" He shook his head. "You don't get down from an elephant. You get it from a duck!" We both laughed. "I know it's terrible!" I said.

Justin's room is right across the hall. He opened his door. "Why did it take three strong Boy Scouts to help the little old lady across the street?"

"Why?" Pete asked.

Jus laughed. "Because she didn't want to go!"

We all cracked up. Even though it was awful. The three

of us just stood there together and laughed our heads off.

"Now, if I can just remember them!" Pete said.

"Why do you want jokes anyhow?" I asked.

"Well," Pete told us, "it's the strangest thing. All of a sudden, the kids think I'm funny! In fact, Jeff's been kidding me about going on TV."

"Let's not get carried away," Justin said.

"It sounds as if you're learning not to take yourself so seriously," I said.

"I don't think I've come to that part of the popularity book yet." Pete grinned.

"Maybe you really don't need the book," I said.

"Well, I'm not *that* confident," he admitted. "Anyhow, for tomorrow it's queens and drones."

"What subject is that?" Justin wondered.

"Science," Pete explained. "I'm doing an oral report on bumblebees."

"Well, what do you know!" Justin smiled. "Birds and bees, without the birds!" He waved and closed his door.

"I'd better get going too," I said. "Good luck! I mean, good luck, *Pete!*"

"Thanks," he said. "I mean, thanks, *Jennifer.*" We both laughed again.

Justin opened his door. "What's so funny?"

"Nothing," I said.

"Nothing, *Justin,*" Pete said. And, although it wasn't *that* funny, we both cracked up all over again.

Chapter 14

On Stage
in Science Class

Lord, it's me, Jennifer.

Personally, I thought Pete really looked handsome! I even said so.

"You're just trying to make me feel good," he said.

"May I give you some advice?" Mom said.

"It depends," said Pete.

"Depends on what?" Mom asked.

"Oh, just tell me what it is," my brother said. "Do I have to follow it?"

"Good grief!" Mom said. "Forget it!"

"Go ahead and tell him," I suggested. Blessed are the peacemakers!

"Pete, when someone gives you a compliment, just accept it and say 'thank you,'" Mom said.

It was good advice. At least, I thought so. "There's this

girl in gym," I said. "She has great clothes. But whenever anyone says 'I like your skirt,' she always puts herself down. Like, 'Oh, I've had this for ages.'"

"I guess I'm not used to getting compliments," Pete said.

"Well, you'd better get used to it," I smiled. "You look awesome!"

My brother smiled. "Thank you," he said. He learns fast.

"I like your hair," Mom told him.

"Thank you, Mom," Pete said.

"I do believe he's got it!" I sang. Pete just looked at me. "It's a line from a song in 'My Fair Lady,'" I said. "See, these English guys were teaching a girl to speak correctly."

"Pygmalion," Pete said. "I read the play."

"Oh," I said. "Whatever. I've got to go. Good luck today!"

"Thanks," Pete said.

Heidi looked all excited when she got on the bus.

"OK, what's up?" I asked.

"They've got this special on earrings at the mall," she said. "Any girl who gets her ears pierced Thursday through Saturday gets an extra pair free." She looked right at me. "What do you think?"

"I think it sounds like a good deal. Are you going?"

"I was sort of thinking we could do it together," she grinned. "How about it?"

"To be honest, I'm chicken," I admitted. "I can't believe I'm saying this. I've been waiting for years for permission!"

"I never wanted to before," Heidi said. "When all the other kids were having their ears pierced, I really wasn't interested in how I looked."

"I got some pierced earrings for Christmas, " I admitted. "But then I went to Haiti."

"So, how about tomorrow?" she asked. "Mom can take us. Can you get away from riding Star for a day?"

"No problem. Do you think it hurts?"

"It couldn't be too bad," Heidi said. "Most people seem to live through it. And they couldn't all be braver than you."

It sounded reasonable. "You're on!" I said. "We'll be sensational at the basketball game!"

"At first you have to wear the little balls," Heidi said. "It takes a while until you can graduate to other earrings."

"Well, with our haircuts, even the little balls will look good, don't you think?" She did.

* * * * * * * *

I thought about Pete only once during the day, and that was at lunch. Before the Winter Carnival, the cool girls didn't want to eat with Heidi. Now, since she was Carnival queen, even Linday and Stephanie sit at our table. Personally, it irritates me. But Heidi always has been nice to them. That's just the kind of person she is.

Anyhow, I'm off the subject again. My point was that Allison complimented me on my haircut. I was just about to protest that I got it ages ago and that I really need another, but then I remembered this morning. "Thank you," I smiled. And that reminded me of Pete. Lord, I said to myself, he's trying so hard! Please help him! Suddenly, everyone was looking at me. Why? I mean, it wasn't as if I had closed my eyes. Nobody even knew I was talking to You. Did they?

"Hey, Jenny," Lindsay said. "I just asked who styled your hair."

I told her his name. "By the way," I said, "please call me Jennifer."

"You don't seem to mind it when the boys chant *Jenny* on the bus."

She had a good point. And good points are problems. Like the rest of my family, I'm big on being *fair.* "The guys are a whole group," I said. "I can hardly make a scene on the school bus." There, that would handle it. Wrong!

"Personally, I think *Jenny* is kinda cute," Lindsay said. "What do the rest of you think?" Talk about dumb conversations! Here we all were eating our hoagies and discussing whether my nickname was "cute!" Finally, Heidi said, "Hey, it's her name. If she prefers Jennifer, I don't see why we can't call her that!"

Well, Heidi had a good point too. And, for the time being at least, that discussion ended. We went on to discuss whether Mr. Hoppert was being mean to make us write so many themes. This time I kept my big mouth shut. Mr. Hoppert would jolly well have to defend himself.

"Thanks, Heidi," I said, as we stacked our trays.

"What are friends for?" she said.

* * * * * * * *

After school I took the bus to Twin Pines. Star was waiting for me. I think he's as excited about being in a horse show as I am! Since Chris didn't come, Star and I spent our time practicing.

"Hi, I'm home!" Dad said when he picked me up.

"Welcome back," I said. "How did it go?"

"Tough," Dad said. I couldn't believe it. Dad has always been on top of things. Confident. Saying things like, "Look on the bright side," and "Every cloud has a silver lining." Well, You know what he's always been like!

"Bad flight?" I asked. That I could handle.

"No. The flights were fine." He sounded so tired. "They've brought in a new man. He's just a kid, really. And he has some different ideas about how to do things."

I felt a knot forming in my stomach. I was beginning to realize two things—that having a job could be hard, and that my father was human. Neither thought was especially comforting.

"We've missed you," I told him.

"I'm glad." He smiled. And, suddenly the world was

OK again. "What's new around here?"

"Pete's got another new image," I said. "I think you'll like this one better!" Dad didn't say anything. But he looked like he was thinking important thoughts.

And then we were home. And Mom and Dad were hugging each other. And I felt even better. The world really is OK.

I headed up for my shower. The first clue I got that something was wrong was Pete's closed door. Well, so he wanted some privacy. He's entitled.

As I stood in the shower and enjoyed the hot water, I remembered Haiti. After vowing that I'd never take pure water for granted again, I've been doing just that. Forgive me, Lord!

I slipped into clean jeans and started downstairs. As I passed Pete's room, something made me knock. (Was it You? I'm just curious!)

"Who is it?"

"Jennifer," I said. "May I come in?"

He let me in and then closed the door after me. "Hi, Jennifer," he said.

"Are you OK? Is something wrong?"

"Not really," he sighed.

"Oh, come on. You can tell me." I took a guess. "Was it the haircut?"

"No. In fact, I got several compliments."

"What then?" I asked.

"My oral report on bumblebees." He certainly was acting strange.

Oh, no. "You didn't use the *zzub, zzub* joke, did you?"

"Huh uh," he said. "but everybody laughed anyway."

"What do you mean, everybody laughed?"

"My talk wasn't supposed to be funny," Pete said. "And I worked so hard preparing. I really was trying for an A."

"So everybody laughed," I repeated. "What was funny?"

"That's the point, it wasn't." He looked very serious. "But everybody took things the wrong way. And they laughed at everything I said."

I couldn't believe it. "What did you do?"

"I couldn't remember what to do," Pete said. "I just got embarrassed. And then they laughed even harder."

"Where was your teacher when all this was going on?"

"She was there. I think she thought I was either encouraging them or trying to be a clown." Pete looked mad. "She gave me a B."

I didn't know what to say. We all want life to be fair, but sometimes it isn't. "Well," I said, "there's nothing wrong with a B."

"I could have gotten a B with a lot less work," he said.

"Think of all you learned!"

"Shut up!" he said.

"I deserved that," I admitted. "I'm sorry. And I'm sorry the kids laughed."

"I'm sorry too," Pete said. "It isn't your problem."

Just then Mom called everybody to dinner.

* * * * * * * *

Well, Lord, that isn't entirely true is it? I mean, that it isn't my problem. When someone in the family has a problem, we all feel it.

By the way, have You had much experience with comedians before? Like, was Bill Cosby always funny? Even when he was in sixth grade?

Chapter 15

What Happened This Evening

Lord, it's me, Jennifer.

"Pot roast! My favorite," Dad announced. "Restaurant food gets old real fast."

"I'd like to try it for a while," Mom smiled. "It sounds pretty good to me."

"Believe me, a business trip is not a vacation," Dad told us. She has heard that before. Every single time he goes. I wondered if he told her about the new man in the company. From looking at them, I couldn't tell.

"Now, Haiti!" Justin said. "That's a vacation!"

"Well," I said, "not exactly. Mom, did I get a letter?" She shook her head.

"How was your day, Mom?" Pete asked.

"Funny you should ask." She had a twinkle in her eye. "The insurance company called. They want me to work three days next week!"

"No kidding!" I said. I smiled at her. "Hey, no tests!"

"Are you sure this is what you want?" Dad asked.

"No," Mom said. "But if I wait until I'm sure, I'll never try anything."

"Will we be latch-key kids?" Justin wondered.

"Of course not," Mom told him. "You have basketball practice every night anyway."

"And I have Star," I said.

"And I'll have to find something," Pete said. "With Mike so heavy into sports, I feel like I've lost my best friend."

"Who'll cook the pot roast?" Dad asked.

"We'll work it out," Mom told him. She's big on schedules. I'd bet anything she's been thinking ahead. "I told my new boss I can't work Thursday afternoons. I don't want to miss our neighborhood Bible study."

"How's that going?" I wondered. She hadn't talked about it lately.

"Fine," she said. And then she smiled.

I kept waiting for Dad to say something about Pete's new clothes and haircut. But he never did.

"Heidi and I are getting our ears pierced tomorrow," I announced.

"Congratulations! Two more holes in your head!" Dad teased.

"Maybe I'll go along," Pete said. Dad turned white.

But he still didn't say anything, so Pete asked him, "Like my new image, Dad?"

Dad smiled. A big smile. "I'm getting paranoid," he said. "I don't know whether to say anything or not. Are you really Pete, my eldest son?"

"In person!" my brother said. "Dad, do you think I'm funny?"

Dad just looked at him. Then he grinned. "So far I haven't noticed much to laugh at tonight. Now, last week!"

"Man, you didn't laugh last week," Pete said.

"I had my *father face* on last week," Dad admitted. "But I was laughing on the inside. Did you want me to laugh?"

"Not really," Pete admitted.

All in all, it was a great dinner! Mom had even baked a pie. Banana cream! I couldn't believe it. She hasn't baked a pie in ages.

"I have a question," Dad said. "Is this pie the end of life as we have known it? Or is it the promise of things to come?"

"What do you think?" Mom laughed.

Personally, I wish she had answered the question, because I wasn't sure either.

* * * * * * * *

The first phone call of the evening was from Matthew. My brothers groaned and headed upstairs. Mom and Dad went into the family room.

"Hi, Matthew," I said.

"Hi, Jenny." I couldn't believe it. It did sound *cute*.

"How come you're calling me that?" I asked.

"You don't like it?"

"Well," I said, "I'm kind of used to being called Jennifer. I've been called that all my life. Probably because it's my name."

He laughed. He has the nicest laugh. "I met the owner of the hardware store this afternoon," he said.

"How'd it go?" I held my breath.

"He's taking me on as an apprentice!" Matthew sounded pleased.

"What's that?"

"I'll be learning to mat and frame pictures," he explained. "Then when Mark goes to college, I'll have the job!"

"That's great!" I said. I decided I wasn't going to bring up the subject of Megan.

"Of course, I won't get paid much for now, but Dad says it's always good to have a trade to fall back on later."

"I'm sure he's right," I agreed. It sounded reasonable.

"The tutoring wouldn't have been good anyhow," Matthew said.

I couldn't have agreed more! "Why?" Frankly, I don't know what made me ask.

"A little matter of temptation," Matthew said. "I think Megan likes me—you know, *personally*. Mark reminded me that a Christian isn't supposed to get himself into situations that could be tempting."

118

"Maybe somebody else could tutor her," I said. I had to say something.

"I'm sure somebody else can," he said. "I was stupid not to see that in the first place."

Well, of course, he was absolutely right! But we all have blind spots. "I'm glad about the job," I told him. Boy, was I glad!

"One of the hard things about not being athletic is not having something to do after school," Matthew said.

I couldn't believe it. "That's what Pete just said," I told him.

"Well, a person can help manage a team," Matthew explained, "but somebody else was chosen. Of course, there's band. But my one summer on the tuba was all the Harringtons could take."

"Pretty bad, huh?"

"Awful." He laughed. "And there's drama. Drama's good. I doubt if I could act, but I probably could have helped with scenery or something."

"But you didn't?"

"No. I got into class politics. And, of course, I've always been active in youth group at church."

"How's the Valentine Party coming?" I asked.

Well, by now a line had formed near the phone. Justin was pointing to the clock, so I said I had to go study. Well, it was true anyway.

Later, the knock on my door was Pete. That figured. I was trying to figure out how to suggest that he go out for drama, but it didn't work into the conversation.

"I'll be at the mall tomorrow, too," Pete said. "Jeff and I and some of the cool kids are going together."

"Does Mom know?" I asked.

"Sure. She trusts me."

"What's that supposed to mean?" I wondered.

"Jennifer, I get awfully tired of your mothering me," Pete said. "You aren't in charge."

"Sorry," I said. "Maybe Heidi and I will see you there."

"I know," Pete grinned. "You'll be the ones with holes in your heads!"

"You've got it!" I said. "I'll also be the one scared half to death! I hope those little balls are totally awesome in my ears! Otherwise this isn't worth it!"

Pete did his chicken imitation. We both laughed. At least he went back to his room with a smile on his face.

Lord, at least it sounds like he's getting popular. Thanks for Your help! But how come he got that B?

Also, thanks for Mom's job!

And for Matthew's job at the hardware store. Which, as You know, gets him away from Megan. Was that Your idea?

Please encourage Dad. Help things at work to go better.

And bless Kirlene and everybody in Haiti—the ones I know, and the ones I didn't meet. In fact, while You're at it, bless all the people in the world who are hungry. That isn't too much for You, is it?

Well, this does seem insignificant. Compared to world

hunger, that is. But help me to be brave when I get my ears pierced tomorrow.

Amen.

Oh. I forgot Justin. I'm not even sure what he needs right now, but I know You know. Thank You that he knows You. Does he tell You all this same stuff?

Good night, Lord.

P.S. I love you!

Chapter 16

Afternoon at the Mall

Lord, it's me, Jennifer.

I can remember when my biggest goal in life was getting my ears pierced! Honestly, I feel embarrassed to even admit it. Talk about immature! Is that the way it is with lots of things? I mean, do You know all along that people's values will change?

Heidi told me something I've never forgotten. It was back when we were really getting into clothes. "God has given us everything to enjoy," she said. "But only Jesus satisfies!" Is that in the Bible?

Well, of course, my point is that after school Heidi and I went to the mall. Everybody wanted to get in on the earring sale, so we had to wait forty-five minutes.

"I wish we could just get it over with!" I told Heidi. We were sitting on a bench and eating frozen yogurt. "Aren't you scared at all?"

She wasn't. I couldn't believe it. "I get scared about other things," she admitted.

"I'd never have guessed," I told her.

"That's because the Lord takes away my fear," she told me. "He's a specialist in handling fear!"

"Is that a fact? I prayed about this last night," I said.

"Really? What happened?"

I thought a minute. "I'm not actually as scared as I thought I was!" I said, realizing it was true. "I've just been afraid such a long time that I didn't know it was over with! What do you know?" I laughed.

"Hey, isn't that Pete over there?"

It was. He was over in front of a department store with a group of guys.

"How's he doing?" Heidi asked.

"He's into popularity," I told her. "Actually, he *looks* more normal. I think the whole family's glad his punk stage has passed. Especially Dad."

"Are those guys his friends?" Heidi asked.

"Beats me! To be honest, I've never seen most of the kids in his class."

"We're next!" Heidi said. The woman in the Piercing Palace was motioning to us.

"Here goes nothing!" I said.

Heidi went first. I wanted to watch to learn the ropes. The woman put marks on her ears and showed her in a mirror. "How does that look?"

Heidi asked me. Well, what do I know? So I said it looked fine.

"You want to pick out your earrings with me?" Heidi asked. Our first choices were little gold balls or little silver balls. We picked silver.

"Actually, they're white gold," the woman explained. "We use gold because there's less chance for infection. The main thing is to keep your ears clean."

The woman held this thing by Heidi's ear. Pow. Pow. And Heidi was grinning from silver ball to silver ball!

I stepped up confidentially to get the marks on my ears. Frankly, I never realized before that people's ears are really quite different. Like, mine stick down farther. Well, You've probably known it all along.

Pow! The noise startled me. Pow! And then, as You know, *I* was grinning from silver ball to silver ball. Heidi and I laughed like ninnies and hugged each other.

Next, we got to pick out our extra free earrings. There were a lot to choose from—even religious ones—crosses, and praying hands, and Bibles! But I picked small silver hoops. I hope You aren't offended.

Heidi got some that the woman called a lover's knot. "Maybe no one will know," Heidi whispered. "I think they're pretty."

We each had to buy a plastic bottle of ear cleaner. We are supposed to remove the little earring holders in the back of our ears, wipe our ears with cotton dipped in the liquid, and turn the little ball a quarter of the way around every day. For six weeks!

"This is going to take longer than I thought," I told Heidi. "I'll have to get up half an hour earlier!"

"Do it before you go to bed," Heidi suggested.

We had just finished paying, when Pete came running up.

"You aren't!" I said. "Pete, please don't!" Personally, I think it's disgusting when guys wear earrings. And I don't care who knows it!

"What are you talking about?" Pete asked. And then he realized what I was thinking. "No way!" he told me. "Hi, Heidi!"

"Hi," she said. "Notice anything different about us?"

"You both look real cool!" he said. "Especially your ears! How about a frozen yogurt to celebrate? My treat."

I nearly fainted. "Thanks, but we just had some. Where are your friends?" I asked.

"It's a long story," Pete replied. "I was wondering if I could ride home with you?"

"Sure," Heidi told him. "Hey, if you want a frozen yogurt, we'll sit with you. Mom won't be here for fifteen minutes."

"He sure looks good," Heidi whispered. We sat and waited while Pete was getting his yogurt.

"Where are your friends?" I asked when he came back.

Pete glanced at Heidi. "No offense," he said, "but I don't feel like talking about it. It's kind of private."

Heidi smiled. "I understand."

"Hey," Pete said, "an interesting thing happened at school."

"What?" I asked.

"You know, Miss Hatcher, my science teacher—the one who gave me the B on my oral report—" I nodded. "Well, today she asked to see me after class. She's directing the school play. And she suggested I try out for a part!"

"No kidding!" I said.

"Well," Pete grinned, "they need a tall guy. And most of them play basketball. I told Miss Hatcher I hadn't done anything like acting. But she said that anybody who could make bumblebees that funny had to have some dramatic ability!"

"I can't believe it!" I laughed.

"Well, Miss Hatcher thinks I'll be perfect."

"Did you tell her you'll do it?" Heidi asked.

"Uh huh. So she said to be at practice after school on Monday." He grinned at me.

"There's more?" I asked.

"You'll laugh," he said.

"Try me."

"I complimented her. I told Miss Hatcher she had pretty eyes!" Well, he was right. I did laugh.

"Did she change your grade to an A?"

"No," he said. "But she did say I made her day!"

* * * * * * * *

Heidi's mom stopped at the entrance to our lane. "See you tonight," I told Heidi.

"Do you think Matthew and Mack will notice?" she said.

"Notice what?"

"Our earrings! What else?" I had forgotten already!

Pete and I walked slowly toward the house.

"Do you want to tell me what happened? You don't have to," I said. "I'll understand."

"I want to tell somebody, Jennifer. You're probably my best bet," he said. "Can you come to my room?"

I wasn't sure if that was a compliment or not. But I said I'd come.

He closed his door. "It was awful," he said.

"Can you start at the beginning?" I suggested.

"Well, there's these guys in my class. Jeff is one of them. And they have kind of a clique. They think they're really cool. And I wanted more than anything to be part of that gang."

"But you weren't?"

"Of course not. They're the ones who called me Saint Peter. Does that sound like I belonged?" he asked.

"I guess not," I admitted.

"They were making fun of me! I told you that before," Pete reminded me.

"Right!" I said.

"So I tried everything to get them to like me. I dressed like Jeff, but that didn't work. And, then I studied how to be popular," he said. "But they didn't start accepting me until they decided I was a comedian."

"I get the picture!" I said.

"So today I became part of the gang." Pete looked miserable. "It was what I thought I always wanted."

"Right!" I said. "And?"

"Well, after school Jeff's mom drove us to the mall," Pete told me. "I thought it would be great just to be with those guys, but, to be honest, it was boring. I mean, one guy even suggested we try shoplifting. That's how boring!"

I took a deep breath. "You didn't did you?" I asked.

"Of course not," Pete said. "I told them it's against the law, which they already knew. So we were just wandering around. That was when we saw Walter."

"Walter?"

"He's a kid in our class. Nice guy, really, but he's very fat." Pete was talking very slowly now.

"So," I said, "you saw Walter."

"He was standing there all alone. Looking at sweaters." Pete turned away for a minute.

I didn't say anything.

"Jennifer, it was awful," Pete said. "The guys started calling Walter 'Hippo.' Always before, they only did it behind his back. Well, anyhow, Walter ignored us at first. But they kept saying it. *Hippo. Hippo. Hippo.*"

I waited, feeling Walter's pain. And I don't even know him.

"Jennifer, it was awful." Tears were filling Pete's eyes. And mine. "Walter just stood there and looked at us. And then he started to cry." Pete was sobbing. "I didn't know what to do. I wanted to help Walter, but I thought it just might make him even more embarrassed."

Tears were running down both our cheeks. Pete

129

couldn't say anything for a few minutes. "Finally, Walter just looked at us, turned, and walked away."

"You hadn't teased him?" I asked.

"Of course not," Pete said. "But still, I was part of it. Part of *them!* And all of a sudden I couldn't stand it a minute more! I told the guys I had to meet you."

"I'm glad we were there," I said. "Are you feeling better now?" I blew my nose and handed Pete a Kleenex.

"I guess so," he said.

"What do you think you're going to do now?" I asked.

"I'm not sure," my brother said.

"You know, Pete, you're really OK!" I told him.

"You are too," Pete said.

And, believe it or not, I actually managed to leave without giving my brother any advice. I'll bet You nearly fainted!

Chapter 17

Will the Winners Please Stand?

Lord, it's me, Jennifer.

Even though I tried, I couldn't get into the basketball game. That's because I couldn't quite get my mind off Pete.

"Jennifer, are you OK?" Matthew asked.

See? Some things never change. Whenever I'm quiet, people think I'm sick.

I smiled. "I'm fine," I assured him. Then I glanced at the scoreboard to see who was winning. They were. I'm not even sure who *they* are!

The cheerleaders decided to use the time out for a "Go, Team, Go!" I yelled. Loud. It must have helped, because Jonathon Davis stole the ball on the thrown-in and tore down the floor for a layup. Now we were only two points behind.

Lord, is sixth grade harder for boys than for girls? I tried to remember how I felt when I was Pete's age. Insecure, that's how! Maybe Pete will get popular in junior high. Do You think so?

Now, everybody was standing up and yelling their heads off. I stood up and yelled my head off too. The game was tied!

"Steal the ball!" Mack Harrington yelled. He looked like he was just itching to get down on the floor himself. In a couple years, he'll be playing varsity—stealing the ball, making the free throw. And will Heidi and I be here cheering? Will Matthew?

And that's how life goes. A few years later, and it'll be Mike Harrington down there. A couple more, and it'll be my own brother, Justin.

Now, everybody was jumping up and down and screaming. And Mark Harrington was coming back in. The star. His ankle taped and a brave look on his face.

"You can do it!" Mack yelled to his brother.

Now, the gym was hushed. Mark, limping slightly, approached the free-throw line.

Swish! Pause, while my heart stopped. *Swish.*

"We won! Mark did it!" Matthew was hugging me. Frankly, the hug was nothing personal. I mean, I don't think he even realized it was me. I might as well have been a post.

Heidi, the silver balls in her ears shining, was laughing at Mack. "He's lost his voice!" she yelled.

Now, the pep band was playing our school fight song.

132

Naturally, everybody stood up and sang. Even me. Only I was remembering that last year I didn't even know the words. What if my family hadn't moved here? Would anybody have missed us?

"Jenny. Jenny. Jenny." Some of Matthew's friends were teasing him. He didn't seem to mind. Nobody seemed to mind anything. The team had won. And everybody was into winning.

But meanwhile, back at home, Pete needed my help. At least, that's what I was thinking. Naturally, I didn't say anything.

Mr. Harrington had taken his turn driving the four of us. He is just about the best driver of any of the parents. That's because he's super at being invisible. He found us, dropped us off at Reuben's, said he'd be back when we called, and disappeared.

"Let's celebrate!" Matthew said.

Mack tried to agree, but his voice squeeked, and everybody laughed. "Guess I'll have to whisper," he whispered.

Do You know what happens when somebody has to whisper? It's the funniest thing. Suddenly, everybody else starts whispering too!

The waitress looked startled when Matthew whispered our orders. The plain truth was that she couldn't hear him at all. Not with all the noise at Reuben's.

"I guess I'd better speak up," Matthew said, "or we'll starve. And celebrating isn't very much fun when you're hungry."

"You're right," I whispered. He laughed. But when he gave our order in a sort of normal voice, it sounded like he was yelling. Which made us laugh even harder.

We had to bend close to hear each other. To be honest, it didn't really work. Which meant that Heidi and Mack were whispering on their side of the booth. And Matthew and I were whispering on our side.

"I think I'm going to like this," Matthew grinned.

"Were you proud of your brother?" I asked.

"Of course," he told me. "Why wouldn't I be?"

"You never get jealous?" I asked.

"He has his good points," Matthew said. "and I have mine."

"Let's see if I can guess," I whispered. "Mark wins the game. And you're Mr. Popularity of the ninth grade."

"He makes a free throw, and I win the post-game competition!" Matthew has the nicest smile. "You sure look pretty tonight."

"It's the pierced earrings," I giggled. "Or didn't you notice?"

"That's what it is!" He slapped his forehead. Mack and Heidi looked up.

"Oh, no! Heidi too!" He laughed out loud. "If it isn't the Bobbsey twins!" he said.

"Don't mind him," I said.

"We won't," Mack whispered. And then he and Heidi went back to what they were whispering about. Whatever that was.

"Jennifer," Matthew whispered, "what's wrong?"

Now, I ask You. Is that sensitive, or isn't it?

"How did you know?" I whispered.

"I don't know. You just seem to have something on your mind."

I didn't know what to say. My family is big on loyalty.

"Pete?" Matthew whispered.

I nodded.

"Do you think it would help if I talked with him?" A wave of relief hit me! It would be perfect! What my brother needed was to talk with somebody who had gone through life on the wrong side of athletic ability! And Matthew would be just the person to give Pete pointers on popularity! Good going, Lord!

"Oh, thank you, Matthew," I whispered. "That would be perfect! I feel better already!"

I've had quite a few hamburgers at Reuben's, but I can't remember another one that tasted any better! Once the food came, we gave up on whispering. All except Mack.

"For once, you have to listen!" Matthew teased.

"What do you mean, for once?" Mack whispered. Naturally, all the rest of us laughed. He does tend to be more quiet.

* * * * * * * *

At the end of an evening, dropping us off at home is always sort of awkward. What often happens is that Heidi is first, I'm second, and Matthew and Mack end up with one of their parents. Practical, yes. Romantic, no. It's even dumber when my parents or Heidi's drive. Then one of *us* has to ride home with a parent! Of course, we're probably not ready for romance anyhow. But that doesn't stop us from looking forward to Matthew's getting his driver's license!

Well, tonight, while we waited for Mack to walk Heidi to her door, Matthew smiled and held my hand.

"OK," Mack whispered, when he got back into the car.

Soon, when Matthew was walking me up to my door, he asked if he could drop over in the morning.

"I'd hate to have Pete think this was my idea," I said.

"It wasn't," Matthew reminded me.

"Right!" I said. "But he might think so."

"I'll come up with something," Matthew said.

"I thought you weren't an actor!"

"This performance will get me an Academy Award," he grinned. "Trust me!"

Well, I had no choice. "'Bye." I smiled. "See you in the morning!"

*   *   *   *   *   *   *   *

When I got upstairs, Pete's door was open and he was smiling. "Come on in," he said.

"What's going on?" I asked.

"I have to tell you something, Jennifer. I worked it out tonight." He closed the door. "Please sit down."

I sat. I could hardly believe how excited he looked.

"Remember the sermon?" he asked. "The one about the birds?"

I nearly fainted. But I tried not to act surprised. "Sort of," I said, racking my brain.

"Remember in the car when Mom said she was a bird snob? That she didn't put much value on sparrows?" he asked.

"It's coming back," I said.

"Well," Pete told me, "I was sitting here thinking—trying to figure out why my plans have been going wrong."

That approach was Pete, all right. I nodded.

"Well, suddenly, I realized that I don't place any value on any birds! To me, birds are a big zero! I couldn't care less."

Surely, this was leading somewhere. Where, I had no idea. "Well," I said, "lots of people aren't into birds."

"But that's not the point," Pete explained. "*God* is into birds. *He* thinks they're valuable. And," he smiled, "He said every single person in the whole world is even more valuable!"

"I'm with you now," I said.

"Well, I remembered that Jesus died for the sins of every single person in the world. For Walter. For Jeff. For you. And for me."

"I believe that," I told him. "Do you?"

"I do now," Pete grinned. "Sure, I've heard it every week since we started Sunday school. But tonight I realized how valuable every person really is." His eyes were sparkling. "See, if Jesus says I'm valuable, then I'm valuable! No matter how out-of-it I may feel! And other kids are important too—no matter how they act or how they look!"

I just sat there looking at my brother. I didn't know what to say. I couldn't say something cool like *"heavy, man!"* But I didn't want to sound like a Sunday-school teacher either.

Pete didn't notice my silence. "I was doing the whole thing backwards," he said. "I was trying to change myself on the outside."

"And God has changed you *inside!*" I said.

"I do believe she's got it!" Pete sang.

"It sounds to me as if you're the one who *got it!*"

"Jennifer, thanks for sticking with me," Pete said. "You're turning into a special friend and an OK sister!"

"You know what?" I gave him a hug. "I'm really going to enjoy having you in junior high with me next year!"

Pete hugged me back. "By the way, who won the game?" he asked.

"We did. Naturally!"

Back in my room, I started giggling. You must have a sense of humor, Lord! First the bees, then the birds!

Chapter 18

The Sting

Lord, it's me, Jennifer.

Saturdays at our house are pretty unpredictable. The only thing we know for sure is that it's like a zoo. Which is why I was kind of surprised when I found Pete eating breakfast with Mom. "Where's Dad?"

"He had to go to the office," Mom said.

I started to feel funny again. "Hi, Pete!" I said. "Did you sleep well?"

"Great!" he said. "And this morning I've already done some reading." I was too chicken to ask which book.

"Justin still asleep?" I asked. He was.

"I've got to get groceries," Mom told us. "Once I start my job, I'll have to be organized. Want anything from downtown?"

Nobody did.

"I'll clean up the kitchen," I offered.

"Thanks, Jennifer, that would be nice," Mom said as she put her coat on. She was just about to head out when the front doorbell rang. "Wonder who that could be?"

Actually, hardly anybody comes over. Especially on a Saturday.

"I'll get it," I said. "Well, hi, Matthew! What a surprise!"

"Hi, Jennifer. Is your mother here?" he asked.

Mom went to the front hall. "Don't stand there with the door open," she said. "Come on in, Matthew. What can I do for you?"

"I see you're just leaving," he said.

"Nothing important. Just grocery shopping."

"That's important!" Matthew smiled. "I just wanted to find out how you're doing with your bird watching."

Definitely not Academy Award, I thought.

"I don't see many new birds," Mom reported. "Mostly cardinals, chickadees, and nuthatches. And purple finches and woodpeckers."

"Sounds like you're doing great!" he told her. "Still enjoying it?"

Mom slipped her coat off. "The feeder is fabulous. We have a steady stream of birds all day! If you have time, we could watch a few minutes." He had time.

"I'll bring cocoa," I offered. "Unless you'd prefer coffee?"

"Sounds great!" Matthew said.

"Coffee for me," Mom replied.

"Want to join us?" I asked Pete.

"Sure," he said, giving me a knowing look. "I'm getting into birds myself!"

"How's your feed holding out?" Matthew was asking

Mom. "That's really one reason I came. Dad's going out to get a bag for Mom. I thought you might be getting low." His act was getting better. I was almost convinced myself.

"What's that bird?" Pete asked.

"Oh, I don't know!" Mom said. "I've never seen that one before!" The yellow bird picked up a sunflower seed and flew away.

"What was it?" she asked. "So I can write it down next time."

"A goldfinch," Matthew said. That figured. It was yellow.

"I really could use another hundred-pound bag of sunflower seeds, Matthew," Mom said. "And, if you'll excuse me, I'm going to head out. I'd like to beat the crowds!"

"So," Matthew said, when she was gone, "how are you doing, Pete?"

"Excellent, Matthew," my brother said. "And you?"

"The same."

"I've been reading a good book on popularity," Pete said.

"No kidding! What have you learned?"

"Did you know that lots of people are shy?" my brother asked.

"I've noticed it," Matthew said.

"One reason is that they're afraid of rejection," Pete reported.

"Is that right?"

Personally, I was feeling kind of left out and rejected myself about then. But, after all, this was Matthew's chance to give Pete advice. If he still needed it. There was no way I could let Matthew know what my brother had told me last night. So I just sat there.

"Everybody's important, Matthew," Pete said. "One of the things a shy person can do is not be afraid to make the first move. Reading helps a person have something to say. And, naturally, being a good listener is important."

Matthew looked surprised. "All that's in your book?" he asked.

"Sure," Pete said. "You can borrow it sometime if you want to."

"Thanks, Pete!"

"Matthew, I hear you're going to start learning picture framing!" Pete continued. "Have you done anything like that before?"

Well, Matthew was right in the middle of telling Pete about his handyman jobs when Justin came down. In his pajamas. "Who's here? Oh, hi, Matthew!"

"I'd better be going," Matthew said. He stood up.

"I was just heading for the kitchen," Pete told him. "Why don't you and Jennifer just watch the birds?"

"Another time," Matthew said.

Pete disappeared with Justin into the kitchen.

"He seems all right to me," Matthew said. "In fact, I couldn't get in two cent's worth of encouragement!"

"He *is* OK," I said. "It's a long story. Maybe I can tell you later. Anyhow, thanks for being willing to help."

Matthew smiled. "You're welcome! And there was a bonus. I did get to see you!"

Halfway down our lane, he turned and waved. I waved back and closed the door.

I was loading the dishwasher when Justin left to go upstairs to get dressed. Pete walked in and handed me the cocoa cups.

"Still feeling good, I guess," I said.

"Excellent!" He stood and grinned.

"Want something?" I asked.

"Say, Jennifer," Pete said. "I'm about done with that book on popularity. No offense, but you might want to figure out some way to lend it to Matthew. Or maybe you'd like me to do it. It's OK with me."

I just looked at him.

"Seriously, Jennifer," Pete said. "I think the big guy's shy!"

"Is that right?" I said. "What makes you think so?"

"Well, he obviously wanted to see you. He must have been desperate for an excuse! Pardon me for saying so, but his excuse of talking with Mom about birds was really pretty sad!"

"You think so?" I smiled.

"Really!" he told me. "I saw through that in ten seconds!"

"Well," I told my brother, "not everyone can win an Academy Award!" Then, as quickly as I could, I ran upstairs because I didn't want Pete to see me going into hysterics!